BLACK HAND SIDE

© 2017, 2019 Randolph Walker, Jr.

Image used with the permission of Pixabay.com

ISBN: 9781020001024

45 Alternate Press, LLC
Hampton, VA

BLACK HAND SIDE

STORIES

RAN WALKER

CONTENTS

NOTE FROM AUTHOR

.

"Black Hand Side" was originally published in *Literary Orphan* (the Black Thought Special Issue). "Jessica and the Mattress" was originally published in *Seek It: Writers and Artists Do Sleep*. "An Occurrence at Osceola Avenue" and "Heavy" were both published in *Brilliant Flash Fiction*. "The Voyeur" was published in both *Mothership: Tales of Afrofuturism and Beyond* and *Frightmares: A Fistful of Flash Fiction*.

I would like to extend a special thanks to the editors of these fine journals and anthologies: Mensah Demary, Elaine Batcher, Kim Aubrey, Aurore Lebas, Paul Beckman, Bill Campbell, Edward Austin Hall, and Stan Swanson.

For Torrey—
You're more than a brother.

BLACK HAND SIDE

I had been dapping Kirby for four hours straight, and now all I wanted to do was just slap him in his bug-eyed face. My hand was tired and on the verge of cramping up like an arthritic crustacean claw.

"One more time, man," he said, massaging the palm of his dapping hand with his other hand.

I shook my own hand, flexing it and wriggling my fingers. "Okay, but just one more time. I don't think I have anything left."

"A'ight. Go all in this time."

"Kirb, I've been goin' all in the entire time. You just handle *your* business. You were a little sloppy on those last few moves."

Kirby grimaced. "Yeah, I know, man. My fingers are sticking a little on the end."

"Don't sweat it," I offered. "The competition is in two days. Just get a hand massage tomorrow morning and don't do anything until the competition. So no spanking the monkey or any of your other hobbies. This thing is no joke."

Kirby laughed, but he knew I was telling the truth. This dude really needed to learn to be a bit more ambidextrous in his extracurricular activities, because he was starting to look like that kid from M. Night Shyamalan's *Lady in the Water*, all diesel on one side and scrawny on the other.

I counted us off and we went into the handshake for the umpteenth time.

The judges would be evaluating us on originality, intricacy of movements, dexterity, enthusiasm, and smoothness. Each of the categories clearly had a subjective component to it, but a few minutes of watching past winners on YouTube gave us all an idea of what the standard was. In fact, if you still had plans to compete after seeing some of the dudes on those videos, then maybe you really were cut out for it. Most people just gave up and threw in the towel, Sonny Liston bailing out on the corner stool.

Kirby was slightly better the last time, but we still weren't on a Jedi-level with our moves yet. There were a few levels of stank we could still throw on our moves, but we could save those for the actual competition, I figured.

"This is gonna be our year," Kirby said. "People been blowing up my Vine account all week nut-cruising the sample I posted on Monday."

"I told you about posting our stuff on the Net. People'll jack your stuff if you put it out there."

"I only put like seven seconds for the loop."

I shook my head. "How much you wanna bet some wack team is gonna use that in their routine, though?"

"But we got two minutes of material. Seven seconds ain't gonna kill us."

"It better not," I said.

That was Kirby's problem: feeling the need to post everything online. He couldn't eat a spoonful of cornflakes without feeling the need to report it to his legion of followers. Still, I couldn't get too angry with him; after all it was his incessant posting that got us noticed and invited to the Dap Invitational in the first place. In fact, the buzz on social media was that we were among the favorites to take the Big Grip Award this year, the Dap Invitational's version of the Best Picture Oscar.

I told Kirby we'd connect the next afternoon and head on over to Memphis and check into our hotel. He nodded. I nodded.

It was a peace out without the dap. We had to save that for the competition.

———

THAT NIGHT I had a dream my hand was stuck in a silkworm web, and I kept trying to get it free, but the more I moved it, the more my fingers got tangled in it. Finally, I just started shaking my

wrist trying to break free, but my hand was
wrapped in white strands like the countrified version of a Michael Jackson glove.

I woke up in the middle of the night swatting
my hand back and forth, still feeling the tickle of
mummy-like threads sweeping across my skin. It
was official: my nerves were a mess.

The Dap Invitational was the major leagues,
and for small town Mississippi boys like Kirby and
me, this was what we needed to put ourselves on
the map. If we won this thing, we could get in
music videos and maybe a few commercials. Two
years earlier a fast-food chain signed a contract
with the winners—which is how most of us got
exposed to the competitive level of dapping in the
first place.

I remember the first time I saw competitive
dapping. The first thing I thought was that I could
do it blindfolded with a hand tied to an ankle behind my back. It was the most basic greeting used
by black people the world over, so there was
hardly anything special about it. The only people
completely mystified by the art of dapping were
white people who tended to vacillate between
standard handshakes and enthusiastic high fives.

Of course my first assessment was a bit over-
simplified. Sure, most black people coded daps
into their greetings on the regular, but very few
people took the time to choreograph intricate
hand maneuvers that lasted for more than a few
seconds. The average competitive dapper had rou-

tines around two minutes, which was actually a part of the guidelines issued by The Dap Invitational. After a little research I discovered that they had to implement the time limit five years ago after a team from Decatur, Georgia, cycled out a "looper" handshake for almost an hour. A looper was when a handshake repeated over and over after a certain number of movements. This was banned by The Dap Invitational, alongside encrypted gang handshakes, which were immediate grounds for disqualification.

Kirby had become my partner, mainly because he was the smoothest dapper I knew in my immediate circle. He could make some of the trickiest moves seem like they were effortless. Kirby was to dapping as Michael Jackson was to moonwalking. And he took it seriously, too, which appealed to me, since I wanted to team up with someone who had a hunger on par with my own.

When we first started practicing, he would have his hands moisturized to high heaven with some dermatologist-recommended collagen-based cream that made his hands sticky and clammy. I had to shut that down immediately. For hands to move efficiently, there needed to be some sense of friction present, and his heavily hydrated hands, while full of dexterity, were freakish in nature when you had to interact with them for longer than two seconds. It felt like his hands had been sweating. But he later took to covering his hands in talcum powder before practice, his compromise with me, since he had no plan to stop greasing himself up. I, on the other hand, would hit my hands with a little Purell ahead of time, so by the time I got to practice, my skin had dried a little to give me a little ash, which was always good for friction.

After a half hour, I lay back down and closed my tired eyes. *No silkworms*, I thought, moving my fingers rhythmically against the sheets. *No silkworms*. Please.

———

MEMPHIS WAS NOT the Promised Land, but it was a step towards it.

I imagined Kirby and myself one day on the largest, grandest stage, elevated before the world, our brand of Negro Exoticism the flavor du jour, the toast of Parisians and Amsterdamians alike. We would be analogous to the South Korean b-boys who routinely whipped the world's collective ass in international break dance competitions.

As we drove up I-55 North listening to Big K.R.I.T. (our theme music for getting ourselves hype), I noticed Kirby in the passenger seat of my hatchback, his hands covered in gloves like Rogue from The X-Men. The way he held them to his chest was as if he were preparing for surgery. I could picture him saying, "We need 50 cc's of saline. She's crashing!"

"How are your hands feeling?" I asked.

"They feel real good, man. We're gonna kill it. Trust me."

"That's what I wanna hear."

I moved my fingers in rhythm across the steering wheel. My hands felt loose and easy. I had almost decided against getting my hands massaged earlier that morning, but it proved to be a good move after all. I figured I was as good to go as I would ever be. It was just too bad that we had to wait one more day to show our stuff.

"You know what's funny about The Dap Invitational?" Kirby asked.

"What?"

"It's, like, the last bastion of blackness left for us. Everything else has been taken over by other ethnic groups. When the Belgians won the Spades Open Tournament or when the Vietnamese took us to the bank in dominoes, or even the Chinese sealing the deal at the Cee-lo Tournament, black people have been losing out on stuff we used to dominate. It's like there's an Eminem or Yao Ming in every black game the world over."

"Well, the name Cee-lo actually comes from the Chinese."

"Man, how do you know all this miscellaneous stuff?" Kirby said, shaking his head. "You know what I mean, though. Hell, if there was a big dick contest, someone not black would take that, too."

I laughed. "You remember that video of the

tribal dude wrapping his johnson around a pole and lifting boulders and stuff with it?"

"No way! I don't think I could handle that. There're just some things that shouldn't be attempted."

While we laughed, I could understand what Kirby was getting at. Still, it seemed inevitable that someone from a different ethnic group would eventually win even The Dap Invitational. It had yet to happen, but that only meant that the sport was primed for a "first."

"Well, if we're the best," I said, "then we shouldn't have anything to worry about, right?"

Kirby nodded.

We drove on to the hotel, each of us imagining ourselves standing on the first place platform waiving the giant $50,000 check before the news cameras.

It was our time—and we knew it.

———

WE WERE PERFECT.

Every finger in sync.

Our arms were fluid extensions of hands that were married in movement like mating eagles falling from the heavens.

It was like we invented dapping, like we were the true originators of the art.

That's what made our loss so confounding.

To add salt to the wound, the Big Grip Award

winners of The Dap Invitational were a group of
countrified white boys from Kentucky. Those guys
actually showed up with sleeveless white t-shirts
featuring the Confederate flag, their pants sagging
off their asses, revealing boxers with more Confederate bars and stars. They looked part Klan, part
thug—and I'm not trying to say they weren't
good, but they weren't great either.

Kirby claimed we had been robbed, that the
judges were determined to let the one white team
win. "What is this? Reverse affirmative action or
something?" he yelled as we walked back to
the car.

"Is that a thing?"

"Well, if white people can claim reverse
racism, why can't we claim reverse affirmative
action?"

I shrugged.

"They did a Macklemore/Kendrick Lamar on
us, dude. Textbook okie doke."

We drove back across the Mississippi state line
in complete silence, the radio off. I didn't know
what to think of what happened. Were they really
better than us? I tried to flip everything in my
mind and see it the way the judges, a primarily
black panel, would have seen it. Was it impressive
that they were white and hanging in there? There
had been white teams in the past, and this one—
at least to me—didn't seem any more impressive
than the others. These dudes had even ended their
dap with the stereotypical high five.

Were they signifying with their handshake?

Could white people really signify?

Could black people continue to ignore the fact that we didn't really own anything anymore?

I still believed we were the better team. But I was biased, I knew.

With the blackness of the night washing through the car, blocking out our ability to see anything other than the highway centerline in front of us, I looked over at Kirby.

His gloves were balled up and pushed into the corner of the windshield, his hands elbow-deep in a bag of fried pork skins, his bug-eyed face black and blank.

MY BEST FRIEND IS BLACK

Two weeks before I graduated from Ellison-Wright College in Atlanta, my friend Kyle Smart, who had graduated from Ellison-Wright only two years earlier, offered me a job making roughly six figures. When I asked him what the job would entail, his response was simple: you just have to be a good friend, a good *black* friend.

Before I had even considered talking with Kyle about a job, I had applied to several MFA programs, all of which I had been rejected; I had also applied for entry-level positions at book publishing houses, magazines, and news websites. Then there was the time I took the LSAT for law school, but scored so low I decided not to apply anywhere. With no prospects—and my father warning me that I would only get to spend six months under his roof with a bachelors degree from his alma mater before I'd have to find my own place—I came across an article on the alumni section of our website, where, in his usually cryptic manner, Kyle mentioned that he had a startup that catered to elite clientele and was on track to gross over five million dollars by the year's end.

I had no doubt that I was at the bottom of a long list of applicants when he agreed to meet with me. And while I had hung out with Kyle a lot over the time he was a student, I had not really spoken to him since he had graduated. I had no idea what his company did and could not find anything about it online, but the fact that he agreed to an interview when I had no other leads, I would have accepted anything he had available.

"Remind me of what you majored in," Kyle started, as he sat down across from me at a table in the student union.

"English. English literature."

Kyle pondered this for a moment. He then pointed to my tie. "Blue. Subdued. I like that."

I nodded in response, not really knowing what else to do. My suit was off-the-rack, but it fit decently. The tie was a discount piece from Burlington Coat Factory. For a college student, I figured myself to be professionally dressed, though I was miles from the bespoke suit and power tie-style of Kyle, who, I had to repeatedly remind myself, had only graduated two years earlier. Whatever golden tit he had planted his lips against, I desperately wanted a taste, too.

"Who are your favorite authors?" he asked.

It was a bizarre question for an interview, but I

still didn't know what his company did, so I guess it didn't really matter. I wouldn't have known a soft question from a hard question anyway.

"Ralph Ellison, Gloria Naylor, Henry Dumas, you know. People like that," I responded.

"I know about Ralph Ellison. The other two—are they black writers?"

"Yes, they are."

"Do you only read black authors?" he asked.

I started to say, "That's like asking if I only eat soul food. Of course not!" But I knew better. Hell, Kyle should have known better, too. One thing he knew from his one or two required literature survey courses at Ellison-Wright was that white literature dominated the curriculum, in spite of the school being historically black. And after a person had read everyone from Shakespeare to Faulkner and still hadn't abandoned the major, it seemed only logical that an English major would like at least some of those authors—if not simply respect them. But I kept those thoughts to myself.

"I read everything. Murakami, Franzen, Munroe, Roth, Welty. I don't discriminate," I answered.

"So they are white writers?" Kyle said. "I know Franzen and Roth but not the others."

"Well, Murakami is Japanese," I said, although his expression indicated he could surmise as much. I continued. "I'm a writer, so I try to read as many different authors as I can."

Kyle nodded his approval. "You're probably wondering why I'm asking these questions."

"It's definitely crossed my mind."

"It all ties back to my business." He let this remark resonate for a moment. "Do you know what my business is about?"

"I've been doing a lot of research, but I keep coming up empty-handed."

Kyle chuckled lightly. "It's cool, Zach. Not many people know what I do—which is the way I like it. Only my clients know. But I guarantee it's completely legal."

"Now I'm really curious," I said. "Are you some kind of real life Hitch?"

"You mean like that Will Smith movie?" he said.

"Yeah."

"Hm." He paused and leaned in closer. "Something like that—but I don't deal in romance."

"Well, what do you deal in?"

"Friendships—at least the illusion of them."

"What do you mean?" I asked.

Kyle reached in to his briefcase and pulled out a three-page document. He placed it directly in front of me. "This is the part," he said, "where I have to ask you to sign this NDA—uh, nondisclosure agreement."

I laughed aloud, thinking this was an elaborate hoax, but Kyle wasn't the type to pull off a

hoax, especially one with props included. I
stopped in mid-laugh. "You're serious?"

"You already know that I am. I'm talking
about a thriving business growing in leaps and
bounds. The things I will share with you are
highly confidential, so I have to protect myself.
I'm sure you can understand that."

I looked down at the paperwork, which was
fairly easy to read and understand. It basically swore
me to silence on everything connected to Kyle's business. It was also loaded with litigious language in the
event that my lips ever became even slightly loose.

"Does signing this paper mean that you're
hiring me?" I asked.

"Zach, you're on of the few people I used to
hang out with when I was here. I would hire you
just on general principle."

"So why did you have me do this interview
with the suit and tie?" I asked, somewhat relieved
that I was much closer to moving out of my father's house.

"Taking inventory. All of it. I just had to see
how much work I'd need to do," Kyle responded.

By this time I was so curious I would have
signed the NDA with my own blood. I quickly
removed a pen from my front pocket and
signed it.

"I see you still keep a pen on you. That's
good."

"Well, you know Ellison-Wright men are always supposed to have one on them—just in case we get that million dollar idea, right?"

Kyle smiled. "Truer words have never been spoken." He collected the NDA. "Let's get out of here and go for a ride. Just one more thing, Zach."

"What's that?" I said.

"Keep an open mind."

————

WITHIN MINUTES, we were on the freeway, his 700 series BMW coasting so smoothly at 80 mph that we might have easily been standing still.

"I'm glad you're doing well," Kyle started. "You look good, healthy."

"I try."

"So, I told you before that I'm in the business of friendship."

"Or the illusion of it," I offered.

"Yeah. That's right. Hey, did you ever see that movie *The Wedding Ringer*?"

"Was that the one where people were paying Kevin Hart to be the best man at their weddings?" I asked.

"That's the one. And that's pretty much what I do, except my business has nothing to do with weddings—at least for the most part. What my company does is catered to an exclusive clientele: white men, affluent ones anyway. Have you ever heard the expression "My best friend is black"?"

"Yeah," I said. "It usually comes out the

mouth of a white person who probably only has one black friend—if that."

"Pretty much. Well, if you come to work for me, you would become that one black friend."

"Are there really white people out there who would pay to have a black friend?"

"Pretty much, if you could even call it a friend. Some of these guys have political ambitions or companies and they need to be seen with the occasional black man. And not just any black man either. The guys we seek to supply have to be well-versed in literature—that would be you—as well as politics, religion, sports, and the arts. I have to employ true Renaissance men, men who are often much more intelligent and creative than the white men they will accompany. At the same time, my "Talented Tenth," if you will, gets a certain level of access, while simultaneously being compensated."

I looked out the passenger window, almost too floored to think. It felt a little like he was an intellectual pimp, as if his "Talented Tenth" were escorts, in the traditional sense. I didn't know how to respond.

"I know what you're thinking," Kyle said, snapping me from my thoughts. "You think I'm selling out and that I am luring others to do the same."

"I don't know what I think," I lied. "I can see how someone might look at it that way, though."

"It's really not even that heavy of an issue,"

Kyle responded. "It would be no different than offering someone money to accompany them to an event where socializing will take place."

"Like *Pretty Woman*?"

"This is strictly business, not pleasure. There's no sex, no subservient behavior, none of that stuff. My clients aren't renting slaves; they are renting the pleasure of the company of an intelligent black man. Hell, my men are some of the only black people to whom my clients are exposed."

"Outside of their help," I offered, but quickly regretted for fear that I might have insulted Kyle.

"Brother, don't flatter yourself. Rich white people don't employ black men anymore. We've been replaced by Mexicans. Some of these white guys literally have no connection to black people at all, outside of the shit they see on music videos, reality shows, and sports. Some of my clients are very well aware of their privilege and what it affords them, but they look at it as a burden that only they are intellectually prepared to carry. My business seeks to prove them wrong—or at least give them exposure to those of us who are not intimidated by their trappings."

"And they pay for this?"

Kyle smiled. "As they should."

"So why aren't you doing all of this by yourself, pocketing all the money?" I asked.

"At first I did, but then I got way too much business and had to bring on someone else. You would be my third hire, if you accepted."

I sat there dumbfounded, staring though the windshield at the downtown skyline. We were on our way back to campus, and I knew he would want to know what I had decided, but I wasn't ready to say yes or no yet. My conscious definitely had a few misgivings, but it didn't sound like that complicated a job from a purely pragmatic view. Then there was the money, which I couldn't ignore, especially with my outstanding federal and private loans that were soon to come due about six months out from graduation. I was looking at over $700 a month in just student loan payments, and the only job offer I had was the one Kyle had put on the table.

"Out of curiosity, how would this work?" I asked.

"Well, I would need to create a profile for you and then put you through our company orientation—a kind of twenty-first century etiquette program—aimed specifically at black men."

"I heard that Motown used to do something like that. Didn't their artists do etiquette training?" I asked.

"I think so, but we do it to fill in any gaps—and we all have gaps—that might put us completely out of sync with our clients."

"So we become Stepford Brothers?"

"Cute. We become *marketable*."

———

WHEN WE REACHED the parking lot behind the student union, I noticed my roommate from freshman year strolling across the yard with his girlfriend. He had already accepted an offer with an investment-banking firm in Manhattan. His girlfriend was from Brooklyn, and it looked like his life had lined up perfectly. I almost felt a pang of jealousy until I realized his boss probably paid Kyle to spend time (publicly) with a guy like me. Suddenly—and sadly—I felt a sense of value, an elite-ness, a uniqueness.

"So, Zach, what's it gonna be?" Kyle asked, turning off the ignition.

"I'm in."

———

WITHOUT A LICK OF NEGOTIATING, Kyle put me on his company insurance and started me on a salary of $100,000 a year, with the possibility of bonuses from various clients. Employment-wise, for a recent college graduate, my deal was incredible, but if I got all of this, I couldn't help but wonder how much Kyle would be renting me out for.

I was now a racialized, intellectual whore, but I preferred to think of myself as one of the stones in the bridge toward a more post-racial America (okay, I tried repeatedly—and unsuccessfully—to do that and believe it). At the end of the day, it was just a job, I figured. Once I put a big enough dent in my student loan debt, I could move on to more respectable work.

The etiquette school proved to be fascinating. I had never learned so much about how to dress in my life. He taught me the entire English gentleman code. Then there was the dining etiquette, art appreciation, how to read financial papers, what to focus on when we read *anything*, and even the finer points of both political parties with emphasis paid to the interests of the one percent. I would have found all of this amusing, if not interesting, even if I were not being paid. Furthermore, Kyle conducted pseudo-conversations for the moments when we had to engage in both small talk and more substantive discussions with our clients. Above all, though, we were required to largely mute our culturally-related behavior. No daps, only high fives—and we were instructed to ration those out so that our clients would try harder to impress us. It was like Pavlov's training for wiggers.

I received one single-breast navy blue bespoke suit with a bowtie (which I was taught how to tie immaculately) and a pair of Italian-made brown leather cap-toed Oxfords with a matching belt. The custom dress shirt was white and crisp with French cuffs. The cuff links were monogrammed with my initials, ZM (Zachary Mercer).

My first event was a party in The Hamptons thrown by a sophomore who attended Princeton. The kid's parents owned a mansion just off the water. Apparently, this kid enjoyed rap music made by people he probably feared in real life. I was hired to be there to legitimize his coolness to the ocean of white people he casually referred to as his friends. Interestingly, I was the only black man there. The three black women in attendance ignored me, as they secretly hoped I wouldn't fuck up their own status with the junior one percenters.

I smiled a lot, gave out a few high fives, and tried not to outdance anyone too badly. The one thing that irked the shit out of me, though, was when a number of the guys got drunk and their true colors began to bubble to the surface.

"So, bro, like why can't I say the N-word when Kanye says it? What's up with artistic intent? If Kanye holds out his mic to me and wants me to say it, who should be able to stop me?" one guy bellyached. "I mean, Kwame, you wouldn't mind if I said it, would you?" He looked at me, and I realized that he thought my name was Kwame (must have been the only black name he could remember in his current state).

"First, my name is not Kwame," I said smiling. "Second, I would appreciate it if you didn't say that word around me." (The "around me" part was my compromise, because I knew he was going to say it anyway.)

"Why not?" he asked, clearly emboldened by the alcohol.

"We're cool, right?" I said.

"Yeah, bro."

"Well, it should be enough that I asked you kindly not to do it."

He paused to consider this when another guy watching the exchange escorted him away to get more beer.

At that event, white guys liked me, but white girls *loved* me. I was propositioned several times before the party ended. It took everything in me to decline the Einstein level of brain I would have received. Still, I was at work—and at that time I had not given myself permission to indulge in *all* of the perks of my job. All in all, it wasn't so bad, though, and the events after that were relatively tame by comparison.

Sadly, I had become pretty good at my job, according to Kyle. I was a favorite of a number of clients. I was easy to get along with, and my complexion was dark enough to legitimize their coolness without being dark enough to make them think me more dangerous than they already believed me to be. Kyle was light-skinned, so naturally his clientele was slightly different than my own.

I only mentioned my complexion just now because it played into my biggest project to date: a seemingly benign political performance that would destroy my anonymity and take Kyle's company into new territory.

———

You would have been hard-pressed to find a politician more despised than Blair Falls, a Southern Republican who used his dislike of Obama (and his funding by an anonymous brotherhood of billionaires) to launch the most vicious, hate-filled campaign for the U.S. presidency in recent memory. Still, a despicable character like Blair Falls required a face of color behind him on stage to keep up appearances that he would not return black people back to bondage. This was the task for which I was chosen—and subsequently the situation that brought everything to a head.

Kyle and I decided to prepare for this by training me to sit stone-faced and clap at shit I didn't agree with. After seeing a black woman read a copy of Claudine Rankin's *Citizen* at a Donald Trump rally, we agreed that we would just do the job rather than use the opportunity to be subversive and undermine our client's ridiculous and twisted stump speech. Kyle had other clients, and hell, I needed the job and had already accepted that I had forfeited my "black card."

I would play it straight, and for this feat I would be granted access to one of the stage seats elevated just behind Blair Falls, for everyone to see repeatedly on any news cycle running that evening. All I had to do was look interested and clap enthusiastically when all of the rednecks laughed and fawned over him.

Even Kyle recognized the snake pit he was throwing me into. I could sense his guilt when he gave me one of his Apollo/Rocky pep talks that was just one note shy of being full-on "Eye of the Tiger."

Feeling that I was holding a superior bargaining chip, especially since I knew Blair's people had paid Kyle well, I made an attempt to negotiate my future.

"I'll do this for you, Kyle. It's my job, but I have to be honest: I'm looking to maybe get into a new line of work soon. I'm kind of getting burned out."

"You want this to be your last one?" he asked, his professional façade never shifting.

"It's been real, but I think it's time to move on to a job that sits a little better with my conscious."

"Your conscious? What does that even mean?"

"I feel like I sell out another piece of myself every time I do one of these things, and with this Blair Falls thing, if there's anything left of me, I want to save that for something else." My words were brief and to the point—plus, I had little else to say.

Kyle nodded his understanding. "Zach, I totally understand where you're coming from. But I thought by now you might've seen the bigger picture. I like to use the acronym AMP: access, money, and power. Those are the ingredients that make the world go around. Some of us, just by the nature of our backgrounds, educations, or even skin colors will never have all three of these things in a solid and perpetual way. What we do have, though, is the ability to nibble at these things—and in this country, that can amount to an impressive living."

"So you feel no guilt at all?" I asked.

Kyle stared at me intently. "I refuse to feel guilt for a success I deserve."

It was a wonder he didn't just fire me right then. Instead, ever the consummate professional, he began preparing me for the Blair Falls event. Our split was inevitable, but business came first.

———

I WAS LITERALLY the only black person on the platform and maybe one of three black people in the entire building who was not an employee of the venue. In my company uniform of a suit and bowtie, I stood out against the ocean of white people dressed far simpler than I was. I looked almost like a member of the Fruit of Islam who got lost and wound up in a redneck honky tonk.

As I stood there waiting for Blair Falls's arrival, I said very little to those people around me, who, from their glances, knew—as if that was even something mildly difficult to ascertain—I was not one of them. But no one challenged me. Instead, we, collectively, waited for half an hour until we saw Blair Falls's security escort usher him to the stage.

At 5'9", Blair stood just a few feet from me. While I had nothing in my possession that would cause him any harm, if I were inclined, I could have just reached out and choked him for a good two seconds before I was wrestled to the floor (and likely lynched publicly by the Klansmen masquerading as his supporters).

Blair began to speak. "America was once a great country. My mam-maw would cook us biscuits and molasses early in the morning before we went out to milk the cows."

I had no clue what the fuck he was talking about, but I nodded as if he were dispensing the heaviest of classical political theories.

"See, we all knew each other and everything flowed because everyone accepted the roles they were given. We didn't try to test God's laws with all of this liberal stuff that defies everything our forefathers stood for when they set up this great nation. We were a people about democracy, not socialism!" he shouted to great applause. In my mind, I was still fuming over his "accepted roles" remark, which clearly meant that people needed to "stay in their places."

Blair was widely referred to as a white nationalist-supporting demagogue, so the media would find little surprising about the implied racism, xenophobia, sexism, or homophobia in his remarks.

And there I was—feet from this asshole, a shit-eating grin couched on my face for the cameras lined up from all the major networks.

Blair continued, beating not only the most

conservative of points, but mocking all other possible perspectives. He was committed to a way of
life that existed in Mississippi prior to the 1960s
—and this throng of thousands was eating out of
his hand.

Every word was like a cigarette being put out
on my face, yet I stood there, the receipt on my
loyalties like a noose, my head nodding at his
bullshit like a bobble-head on a dashboard.

By the time Blair concluded his speech and
raised his hand to wave at "his" people, I could
swear his hand appeared to be angled into a Nazi
salute—at least from my point of view.

And then he turned around to face those of us
standing on the platform behind him. He waved,
as he had at the audience in front of him (not so
much a Nazi salute from this angle). Then he
looked directly at me—and winked.

Something in me snapped, and before I could
hold in place that mask of indifference I had been
wearing, I quickly mouthed the words "fuck you!"

I didn't think anyone noticed, but Blair's reaction signaled that I had offended him, and I
quickly felt my feet lifted from the platform as the
white guy behind me wrapped his musty arms
around me, giving me a wild bear hug. I yelled for
him to let me go, and within seconds, I was
buried beneath a pile of rednecks, while Blair casually walked offstage.

As I swung my fists, connecting with jaws and
eye sockets, people began to give me space. Even-

tually, the security guards standing nearby were able to grab both of my arms and dragged me out of the building and onto the sidewalk out front. I quickly ran down the street to distance myself from any crazy rednecks looking to continue the fight.

I ran around a corner roughly half a mile away and inspected myself to see how badly I had been bruised and if anything had been broken. I was okay, just sore and shaken up.

I took out my phone and sent for an Uber car. Within half an hour, I was in my apartment, removing my uniform for the last time, content to let the blood stains dry there.

———

WHEN I AWOKE, I saw that I had missed no fewer than seven calls from Kyle. There was even a text message with a GIF of me on loop, mouthing the word "fuck you" at Blair Falls and then being jumped by a group of white men. His message alongside the image was "WTF?"

I then opened my Twitter app to find the hashtag #FuckYouBlair trending in the number one spot. As I scanned my news feed, I saw memes of me mouthing the words with captions like "When You See the Last Episode of *Lost*." People were having fun using my rage in a variety of ways. I was Angry Man, just like Crying Jordan, just like Uncle Denzel. But then there were a few people who saw what I had done as a bold and unadulterated response to Blair's madness, albeit not the most eloquent.

Just last week I signed a deal with a merchandising company to use my likeness from that image on t-shirts and what-not. I even did a commercial for a website. So, while I am no longer working for Kyle, I feel as though I am somehow still in the game.

I have long since resigned myself to the fact that I have sold out. I am a fifteen minute punch line, and I have already planned to move out of the country by next summer—which I am happy to acknowledge is when I will have completely paid off my student loans.

THE IMPERSONATOR

When I was growing up, adults would often ask each other what they were doing when certain major events took place. They were usually referring to the assassinations of President John F. Kennedy and Martin Luther King, Jr. I was baffled how they could recollect with such peculiar accuracy what was going on around them in those moments. When I grew older, the death of the rapper Hannibal Streets would become one of those "what were you doing when" moments for my generation.

I remember very vividly what I was doing when I heard the news of his passing, mainly because I was preparing to do a stand-up routine at Hosea's Amateur Comedy Night, where I had prepared some jokes about Hannibal. I ultimately decided against telling those jokes—which were largely impersonations—and ended up bombing, although the largely grieving audience was merciful. If I had been a halfway decent comedian, I could have flipped my act that night and used those impersonations to comfort and uplift the spirits of my audience. The shock of the news at that moment, though, impaired my judgment, and I panicked.

A year later I ventured into another open-mic amateur night and did the original Hannibal routine. It got a few laughs, but it didn't completely slay the audience, as I had hoped. Afterwards, however, a few people came up to me and complimented me on my impersonation. Unbeknownst to me at the time, one of those people would eventually take my career to the next level.

————

HANNIBAL STREET'S rise to becoming arguably the greatest emcee of all time started inauspiciously with him serving as a roadie and background dancer for a West Coast rap group called Kilobytes. But you probably already know most of this, since his bio has been rehashed thousands of times by every news source covering entertainment the world over. During his seven years in the music business, he released three platinum-selling albums before being murdered outside of the Super Bowl in 1997. But I'm sure you already know that, too.

Probably one of the most fascinating things about Hannibal was how prolific an artist he had been, especially once he completed a two-year stint in prison for the alleged sexual assault of a beauty queen (an issue relentlessly debated by fans well after he had already served his time). His second album (or first since his release) was a double LP that went four times platinum. His third LP sold nearly six million units. After his death, rumors circulated that he had damn near five hundred songs locked away in some vault, heavily guarded by his record label, Three Strikes. As a result, almost like clockwork, Three Strikes drops a new Hannibal Streets LP each year, showcasing some hot new producer the label is looking to promote.

It's all quite a story, really. It's like one of the greatest emcees of all time never really died (don't get me started on the rumors that he faked his death). This is the public narrative as we know it, and it is the story my daughter, Zina, knows.

But it's not the only story there is.

There's also my story.

———

ON THE NIGHT I was finally able to perform my Hannibal Streets routine, I met a guy name Eli Jones, who introduced himself as the owner of a talent agency of the same name. Roughly 5'5", he was full of confidence and knew just how to approach me to get me to sign on as a client. He gushed over my comedic timing, my choice of material, and my level of comfort in front of an audience. What really floored him, though, was what he referred to as a spot-on impersonation of Hannibal Streets. Up till that point, I had thought my impersonation as just good enough—definitely not spot-on.

"Who you kiddin'?" Eli responded. "I closed my eyes and thought that nigga was still alive."

"Well, you know what some people say," I offered, referring to the conspiracy theorists.

"Whatever, man. What I do know is that you sound just like that motherfucker. Don't look a damn thing like him, but I bet you could fool his mama on the phone."

"Really?" I asked. "Did you know him personally?"

"Yeah, I knew him. That's why I know what the fuck I'm talkin' 'bout."

His interest seemed genuine enough, so I signed with him. I thought he might help me get booked at a few places—maybe set me up for the occasional talk show appearance. That was not his plan for me, he told me. "Let's go make some *real* money."

To me, in my naiveté, that meant an HBO show or something on Netflix, but it wouldn't be long before the I realized who my employer for the next decade would be: Three Strikes Records.

———

BACK WHEN THREE Strikes first started, they

owned one studio at the back end of a shopping center, and most of the music production was done by one person, Infinite Design. In fact, music journalists are quick to point out that the "sound" of Three Strikes was built on the back of that single producer. Hannibal's rise to success was likely accelerated by Infinite Design's beats, but later on, after Infinite Design left the label, Hannibal Streets's voice became the strongest cachet for Three Strikes. I guess the thinking was that they could cultivate a whole new crop of producers as long as they had Hannibal's voice to anchor the tracks.

Once Eli introduced me to the executive team over at Three Strikes, I came to see things a bit differently.

"Eli tells me great things about you," Gamma, the CEO, said, shaking my hand.

I was floored by the compliment. I had never met a black man who was listed on the Forbes 400 Wealthiest Americans list. He could have told me he shit strawberries, and I would have believed him.

"I hear you do a pretty good Hannibal," he said.

"I try."

"Do you know any of his songs by heart?"

"A few," I responded.

"Well, let me hear you spit something then."

I thought for a moment, fighting my nerves with each passing second. I figured I'd just do the latest song I'd heard of Hannibal's on the radio a few weeks earlier.

As I launched into the rap, Gamma's eyes grew larger. He stopped me halfway through the second verse.

"Gotdamn, Eli!" he said. "I thought you was just fuckin' with me."

"I told you," Eli responded. "Sounds just like that motherfucker, don't it?"

Gamma nodded enthusiastically, tugging on his rugged goatee. "Well, then. Let's talk turkey. You wanna call it consulting? How about 100 grand per project?"

"I was thinking more like 150 and a finder's fee," Eli said.

"Hey, what's going on here?" I finally piped up.

"I'm negotiating your contract," Eli said.

"But what exactly am I being hired to do?"

"He don't know?" Gamma said.

"Well, I wanted to wait and see if you liked him first," Eli responded.

"Can someone please fill me in?" I asked.

Gamma looked at me and smiled. "No problem. Let me break it down for you."

Over the next hour Gamma explained everything to me, as Eli stood by, patiently nodding. Apparently, the infamous vault of recorded material by Hannibal Streets, while once voluminous, had all but dried up, yet his album sales were higher than ever.

"At first it was just a crazy theory, since I've never heard anyone sound enough like Hannibal to pull it off," Gamma said. "Son, what I'm offering you is an opportunity. If you're not interested, we never had this conversation. You feel me?"

"Yes, sir," I said, suddenly realizing what was being asked of me.

"*Sir?*" Gamma responded, looking at Ali, yet pointing at me. "I like this little nigga."

Shortly after that meeting, Eli negotiated a contract with me that, due to the sensitive nature of our dealings, would allow me to be paid six figures in cash per LP. The only problem was that, beyond my imitations of Hannibal, I couldn't actually rap to save my life.

———

AS FATE WOULD HAVE IT, I didn't have to be a rapper at all—just a voice impersonator. Gamma had already assembled a small production team of up and coming producers and ghostwriters. The ghostwriters would pen the raps and show me the intonations, inflexions, and rhythms. In many ways I found their roles far more difficult than my own. They were the ones perpetually tasked with going into the creative mind of Hannibal Streets and asking themselves what he might have said and how he might have said it. They had to be both rapper and speechwriter. All

I had to do was imitate Hannibal's voice, but, according to everyone involved, that apparently was the hardest part of the equation. I was told no one had ever mastered Hannibal's uniquely raspy voice and his energetic and rhythmic cadence.

We did nearly one hundred songs before my girlfriend told me that we were expecting. Few things can make you reassess your life like the awareness that you are about to be a parent. Still, I kept on with Three Strikes.

I found doing Hannibal to be fun, a way of stepping outside of my regular life and becoming someone else. At times, while recording, I would not just imitate Hannibal's voice; I would imitate his mannerisms, bouncing on the balls of my feet as I spoke, throwing my arms back and forth so that my body swayed in his familiar rhythms. I would close my eyes and imagine I *was* really him. The producers ate it up. So did the public, as Hannibal's records continued to sell through the roof.

———

IN RETROSPECT, I sometimes feel that the public had to know of our ruse. I was convinced that maybe we all wanted to believe Hannibal had an inexhaustible supply of unreleased material sitting in a vault somewhere. Or maybe the conspiracy theorists were right: Hannibal had in fact faked his death and was now living his life in seclusion out in Cuba or some island out in the Caribbean.

I knew better, but I allowed myself to get caught up in all of it. Even as I saw my daughter growing up beside me, I felt more than a financial obligation to uphold the legacy of Hannibal Streets. His life's work was now my life's work.

And I thought I would always be fine with that.

Then one day my daughter, who was now twelve, came up to me and asked me a very simple questions that I should have long ago expected (but had never gotten) that put me into a bit of a tailspin: "Dad, what do you do for a living?"

I thought about telling her that I was a voice actor or a consultant for a record label or something like that (all variations of the truth), but I found myself unable to really articulate any of these thoughts for fear that she would ask me follow-up questions I was unprepared to answer. I was a man who couldn't answer a simple questions, and sadly, that question gave way to a far more paralyzing question: who had I become?

Twelve hours out of the day I was a father, a guy who rooted for all of the local sports teams, a guy who lived to binge-watch newly discovered TV shows on Netflix. The other twelve hours, though, I was a musical—a spiritual—conduit for one of the greatest emcees to ever live. There was no greater high, except for the day that my daughter was born. During those twelve hours, I

would talk like Hannibal, move like him, even try
to eat like I imagined he would eat. The producers
at Three Strikes gave me the space to inhabit Hannibal however I could, and I did that. I did my
best to become him. The albums kept coming,
and I never took my foot off the gas. I had come
to a point where I had to impersonate the self that
I once was so as to not betray those in my life before all of this began.

I had become a nameless ghost that moved
from voice to voice, body to body, and no one,
not even I, was the wiser. I had lost myself, all
while attempting to become someone I could
never become.

When I approached Gamma about walking
away to start a new life and be a respectable father
to my daughter, I had half-expected him to have
one of his goons beat me to a pulp in the lobby of
Three Strikes. There was definitely a time when he
might have done that, if only to maintain his rep
as the no-shit taking ex-con mogul of a record
company specializing in gangsta rap. But I knew
he wouldn't. For one, the work I did for him was
too confidential to invite any attention. Second, I
had cut him more songs than even Hannibal had,
and the company would be good for at least another decade. But the main reason I knew I would
be able to walk away in one piece was because I
wasn't the only one who had changed over the
years. We all had. Gamma was now spending
more time with his own kids, as his oldest son was

preparing to accept a lacrosse scholarship to Hampton University in the fall.

We parted ways with a half-hug/half-handshake and his insistence that I take another $25,000 for severance.

These days I spend my work hours on the stage at any comedy club that will host me. So Dad is now a struggling comedian, my daughter often says, before adding, "How is that even possible when you're not even funny around the house?"

Maybe not, I think and then smile to myself. It's so hard to know these days what's really funny. Occasionally I want to break out my Hannibal impersonation—go for the lowest hanging fruit—but I resist. That part of my life is now behind me. What lies ahead, though, I am still attempting to figure out.

JESSICA AND THE MATTRESS

Jessica agreed to move in with me on one condition: I had to replace my mattress. We had been dating for two years, and this was the first time she had even mentioned that my mattress bothered her. If she had asked me to replace the bed frame or purchase a new headboard, I wouldn't have hesitated—I might've even understood—but she was asking me to go to the heart of the bed, the part that had seen me through the last ten years of my life, the part that had finally conformed to my body in such a way that I was now enjoying the best sleep of my life. She was asking me to make a sacrifice of incalculable measure.

See, to me, sleeping is more than the necessary recuperation of the body; it's my hobby. Some people collect coins or baseball cards. Others take cooking classes or pick up scuba diving. Me? I sleep. And when I say "sleep," I mean I get down and dirty with it. I own a special pair of socks, a lucky pillow (three smushed pillows squeezed into the same pillow case), and a comforter that my grandmother gave me as a high school graduation gift. I often propel myself through a trying day of working the grill at The Pit over at State University by thinking of how good the sleep will be when I finally get home. In fact, I believe I work even harder so that I can sleep even deeper.

The mattress was the first thing I bought when I moved out of my freshman dorm in college. There was nothing particularly special about it, but years of lying on it every-which-a-way, whether I was sharing it with someone or just lounging alone, broke it in the way an old car might be broken in by its owner. My father's 1993 pick-up truck has nearly 450,000 miles on the original engine, but he is the only one who knows the combination of jury-rigging necessary to get the thing to move down the street without cutting off. Like my father's truck, I am the only one who knows and, more importantly, appreciates the subtleties of my mattress, those lulls in the cushion where the springs have given way and cause you to roll toward the center of the bed.

And now Jessica wants me to abandon this mattress. It's like asking a man to give up being a fan of his favorite sports team, or even give up his religion.

As I stood listening to her request, she said in no uncertain terms that I had a choice to make: her or my mattress. I wish I could say that I labored over the decision—or even slept on it one last time—but in reality my response was reflexive, almost involuntary.

Sometimes I still think about Jessica and miss her dearly, but knowing that I can put on my socks, grab my comforter, and jump into my bed for some of the best sleep of my life, makes the pain much more bearable.

The smart phone was more than three generations old, but it may as well have been fresh out of the box. It was the only luxury he had afforded himself once he left the halfway house and moved into his apartment, several blocks from Howard University. He still couldn't afford to turn on the phone service, but Frank's Burgers had free WiFi, not to mention pretty decent burgers. The restaurant was just off of Dupont Circle, a place where WiFi signals ran strongly, nonstop.

David Stembrook poked at his french fries while combing through a job website he visited each day. His current gig of bouncing at a strip club over on Connecticut Avenue was sure to lead to trouble at some point. Too many of the wrong kinds of people came through there, and he didn't want to get too close to a situation that might cause him to go back to the joint. This was just something temporary so he could send Tasha some money for their daughter, Kara. The website didn't have much posted that day, but he still forwarded his resume to a few places in the city, mainly busboy positions at restaurants, where he had heard they often gave jobs to people like him.

David had been in Frank's Burgers for nearly half an hour before the men and women in suits came into the restaurant, requesting to see the manager. David glanced out the window and noticed several large black SUVs blocking the street in front of the restaurant, with police cars flashing lights on either end of the caravan. Probably some foreign dignitary, David figured. He had been in DC long enough to see how they flaunted their power throughout the city.

A few minutes later, the manager came out and spoke to the handful of customers eating their lunches.

"Excuse me, everyone. The men and women you see here are with the secret service. If you'd like to get your food to go, I can get you set up, but when our guest comes in, everyone will need to remain where they are until he leaves.

"If you decide to stay, I will need to ask you to comply with the instructions of the secret service people here," the manager said, his face perspiring heavily over his reddened skin.

The energy in the room suddenly became electric, and no one made any attempts to leave.

"Who do you think it might be?" a forty-something-year-old blonde-haired white woman asked the older balding black man seated at the table next to hers.

"Secret service? Probably Uncle Joe. This seems like a Biden kind of spot," he responded.

"Wow. That would really be something," she responded.

"It's President Obama," David said, unable to take his eyes off the SUVs.

"How do you know?" the older guy asked him.

"I don't know how. I just do."

"Well," replied the woman, "that would be amazing, wouldn't it?"

Neither David nor the old man said anything, weighing the magnitude of such a possibility.

The secret service team swept the restaurant and then checked each of the handfuls of customers, along with all of the employees, with metal detectors, frisks, and examinations of personal effects.

David could feel his stomach bubbling with gas, a nervousness so unfamiliar to him sitting dead on his midsection. The last time he had felt that way was when Tasha had told him she was pregnant over eight years ago. He was only seventeen at the time and had a year to go before he graduated from high school. At first he was unsure of whether or not Tasha would have the baby, since she had confided to him that she had gotten an abortion when she was fifteen. But with graduation looming for both of them, Tasha had decided she wanted to have the baby.

David didn't know what kind of father he would be. His own father had never been around, and his grandmother had raised him since his own mother decided to chase after some man in Chicago. When he had told his grandmother he was going to be a father, she was not pleased.

"I knew that little girl was fast. Well, I'ma tell you this: I'm not raising no more kids," she said, licking the gums around her dentures.

Knowing he was on his own, he pulled a few burglaries in an effort to build the kind of nest egg that dropping fries at McDonald's couldn't have provided. He was told that the key to burglaries was to be fast, exact, and not carry any weapons (being armed could multiple your sentence if you were caught). And like many people who did things with a bit too much ease, David did one job too many and found himself behind bars, begging Tasha to bring Kara by so he could see the daughter for which he would have sacrificed everything.

He couldn't have expected Tasha to stay with him during those years. After all he knew they had been kids, teenagers who were never really in love, but he had Tasha promise him that he could still be a part of his daughter's life—no matter who she chose to love.

Tasha upheld her end of the deal but married a guy from Arlington two years after David went away. By all accounts, he was a good stepfather, and Tasha made no efforts to collect child support from David, mainly because she already knew he would have given whatever he had to Kara.

The new job search was all for Kara, too. David wanted to be able to do more for her, financially, and for that to happen, he needed a more stable income. He was determined not to get sent away again, so he would do it all on the straight and narrow.

"Sir? The older woman said, her face flushed with excitement.

David turned away from the window to face her. "Yes?"

"Do you think we'll get a chance to meet him?" she said, almost breathless.

"Probably ain't even him," the older guy said. "No point in getting all worked up for someone you ain't gonna ever meet."

Just then, one of the employees bussing a table nearby whispered, "It's Obama," before shuffling away to leave the three customers' mouths agape.

"Well, I'll be damn," the older man said. "We *are* gonna see the president." He immediately picked up his cell phone and began texting someone.

So did the older woman.

David, the youngest of the three—by far—picked up his phone and realized he had no one to tell the news to. He wasn't on any of the social media networks and Kara was too young to have a phone or tablet or any of that fancy Internet stuff, so he would have to silently digest this new update on his own. Now he wondered about the older woman's earlier question. Was it really possible that he would get a chance to meet the nation's first African-American president, a man for whom there seemed to be no ceiling, whereas nearly everything in David's world was a ceiling?

For several long minutes everyone seemed to stare nervously at the black SUVs in front of the restaurant. No one said anything. David didn't want to miss a single moment of President Obama, and from the looks of the customers around him, they didn't either.

If he were to get a chance to shake the president's hand, what would he say? He normally didn't give famous or important people much thought. It was just part of growing up in DC. You couldn't be fazed by stars. They were always in and out of the city.

But this was Barack Obama, and if ever there were an exception to the rule, this was it.

Less than a year ago, he was in a cell wide enough to turn around in and do a few push-ups. It was only large enough to accommodate the small bed that would serve as his desk for writing poetry and raps (his hobby) and reading books he heard about through the inmates who worked in the prison library, writers like Etheridge Knight,

Henry Dumas, and Amiri Baraka. All the time he was in his cell, the hours so late he didn't know what the sky looked like outside, he told himself in almost a full-blown mantra that he would do right by his daughter. He would one day make her proud to call him her dad.

Now he was on the verge of seeing, up-close, a man who had overcome obstacles that made the years David served behind bars seem negligible in comparison. Who was David to be in a position to be there at that moment? What kind of lottery had he won to be at the one restaurant in all of DC that would host the president, if only for a few minutes? Maybe the tide was turning and his life was finally locking into the right direction.

Then he had an idea: he would take a picture of President Obama when he came into the restaurant and find some place to print out the picture from his phone. He would then send the picture to Kara to show her how close he had been to greatness. Maybe a little of President Obama's glow would rub off on him in his daughter's eyes.

"Is he ever getting out of the truck?" the older guy asked. "This is taking forever. I got other stuff to do today."

No one acknowledged the man's remarks. They all knew he was talking big, more than likely to steel his nerves.

Swiftly, the secret service opened the door, and like a bird being set free, President Barack Hussein Obama, Jr. emerged from the back of the second

SUV and floated in fluid, soulful strides into the door being held open by one of the security team.

The detail created a path from the door to the register, but David, who now stood on his chair, aiming his smart phone at the scene, felt the electricity of the air glowing around his entire body. He snapped pictures furiously.

That was when one of the aides who had come in with the president began quietly approaching certain people in the restaurant. When the aide approached David, she asked very directly, "Would you like to shake hands with the president?"

At first David couldn't comprehend the question. It was like the words were in a foreign language. Then his brain woke up and kicked in. "Yes!" he said firmly, unable to conceal his excitement at having been asked.

The aide guided him over to a line that was forming off to the side of the entrance. The older woman and older man were already in the line, and David's arrival was regarded with a warm smile and nod from each of them.

Once President Obama finished glad-handing the employees, making a few jokes, and picking up one of the bags of food for his staff, he made his way quickly to the customers lined up to shake his hand.

In the moment the president started down the line, David was able to hear his voice clearly for the first time. He could see the president perfectly from where he stood, and he couldn't help but take as many pictures as his hand would allow him to take.

Before David knew it, President Obama was shaking the hand of the man right next to David. He was next in line.

Once the president finished shaking the man's hand, he eased over directly in front of David. David looked up into his eyes (how *tall* was he? Definitely taller than he looked on TV) and took in that warm, familiar smile.

"Nice haircut," the president said, taking David's extended hand.

"Thanks," he responded, feeling as if his voice belonged to another body. "I just came from a job interview." And then, totally unexpectedly, he unloaded his life story on the president, confessing that he wanted to do right by his daughter since he'd gotten out of prison, but that it had been a struggle.

He was surprised to discover that the president was actually listening to him, David Stembrook from Northeast DC.

"Arty," President Obama called out, raising his hand. The manager of Frank's Burgers came over quickly. "My young friend here is looking for a job, an opportunity, so he can do right by his daughter. What's her name?"

"Kara," David said.

"Kara," Obama repeated, then looking back at

Arty, "Surely we can find something for this young brother. Can't we?"

Arty nodded, clearly put on the spot. "I'm sure we can find something."

"Good," Obama responded.

"Can I take a picture with you, sir—for my daughter?" David asked.

"Sure."

After the picture, the security detail ushered the president quickly toward the door. In less than a minute, the caravan of SUVs had pulled away, leaving the people in Frank's Burger's dazed and light-headed.

David looked at his phone and began fanning through the pictures he had taken. He could hardly believe what he was seeing. Picture after picture, he relived everything he had just experienced. Now he needed to find someone to help him get prints of the pictures made so he could send all of them to Kara.

"Excuse me, young man."

David looked up. "Yes?"

"I'm Arty, the manager here. Were you serious about a job—just now?"

"Yes, sir."

"Well, let's step back here to my office and talk. I'm sure we could find something around here for you."

David glanced at the last picture, the one of him and President Obama. He smiled. He then put his phone back in his pocket.

"He was really something, wasn't he?" Arty said.

"Yes, sir."

"Well, let's get to it and see if we can get you set up."

"Yes, sir."

THE MIGHTY BIRDS

I t all started one Sunday afternoon when my roommate, Blake, bored with the football game we were watching, decided to break from our weekly tradition and try something new. He called my name, and when I turned to face him, he extended his middle finger crudely, a giant smile on his face. At first I didn't know what to make of it, so I ignored him. But somehow over the course of the next few weeks, we managed to create a game around it, awarding points to the individual who could sucker the other into looking at a fully unfurled bird through some act of embellishment or guile.

Blake created the bird toss, which consisted of him calling out to me, "Catch!" and moving his fist in a tossing motion only to release his middle finger. For effect, he would bob it up and down so that my head could not help but bob in anticipation of whatever I thought he was actually throwing. Then I came back with the pocket bird, which I usually delivered smoothly with a phrase like, "Hold on. I forgot to give this to you this morning," before removing my middle finger from my front pocket.

And there was the "symphony conducting" bird, the "let-me-scratch-my-chin" bird, the "boy scout sign" bird, the "ooh-I-just-touched-something-hot-and-burned-my-middle-finger-so-I-have-to-shake-it-in-your-face" bird, and the classic "take-a-picture-of-yourself-shooting-the-bird-and-snail mail-it-to-the-other-person" bird. By the beginning of our senior year, we had managed to persuade a good thirty people to participate in this ongoing game.

We knew we were being silly, but it was what we did: take something many people found offensive and flip it into something we could make a running joke. I mean, think about it: it was just a person holding up a finger; it wasn't like someone was waving a loaded Desert Eagle in your face.

But even with all of our reckless, rebellious energy, I would have never thought we would ever plot to get the graduating class of 2005 to agree to collectively shoot the bird to our commencement speaker. After all, there had never been a precedent for such a massive bird shoot, let alone one aimed at the President of the United States.

As MUCH AS I usually love to claim credit for masterful ideas, the bird shoot was really Blake's brainchild. The irony of it all is that he voted for Bush—in both elections.

While trolling YouTube, he came across of a video of Bush shooting the bird to a video camera man, all in jest, and apparently the light bulb went off in his head.

"Gerald," he yelled to me from his bedroom. "I have an idea."

With Blake's ideas being legendary, I knew whatever he was going to propose would probably have some stiff consequences. He played the video for me several times before saying, "What if we organize it to where the entire graduating class shoots him the bird during commencement?"

I looked at him like he was wearing Alex's penis-face mask from *A Clockwork Orange*. "You must be high as hell," I finally said.

"Not at all. Think about it. If we did it the right way, I think we could pull it off."

I shook my head. "This is the freaking President of the United States, man, not some frat boy from across campus. They would throw all of us *under* the jail."

Blake looked at me, his lips poked out in an exaggerated manner, his eyes pleading in the way that small children sometimes did with their parents. I just looked at him, unfazed.

"Well, I tell you what," he said. "How about this: we just consider how it could be done if, hypothetically speaking, we actually went through with it."

I knew I would never hear the end of it if I didn't at least agree to play his game. The only problem with Blake and his hypothetical situations was that we often wound up figuring out a way to do something that was so kick-ass that it would have been a shame not to at least try it— just for "scientific purposes."

And so it was with what we came to refer as "The Mighty Bird Shoot."

————

THE FIRST THING we did was tap into the growing Facebook network on campus. Nearly all of the tastemakers had accounts now, so we referred them all to the YouTube video of Bush's infamous bird. Because it all came from us, everyone immediately got the joke. By the end of the week, nearly all of the graduating seniors had seen the video. That's when Blake stepped in with Stage Two. He explained how the bird-shooting game went and how it would be classic if we were to pull off one of the best-organized bird-shoots in history.

All of the pranksters, frat boys, and party people fell right in line, but the other three-quarters of the graduating class were not as sold on the idea. This is where I came in.

After fielding nearly a hundred questions

through my Facebook account, it became clear that they didn't really have a problem with the bird-shoot, as much as they feared being caught participating in it. After all, families were driving long distances for a solemn occasion, not to mention it was still unclear if we could get arrested for doing all of this in the presence of the Head of State.

I didn't know what to tell them in response, except that Blake was working on the idea of how it could be done. "Just hold on and see what he comes up with," I offered, but I doubt that comment did much to assuage their concerns.

For two weeks things dragged along at a snail's pace, and even I began to think Blake couldn't come up with an idea on how to pull it off. That was probably for the better. He was white and his alleged sin could be explained away through youthful playfulness. My being black, on the other hand, meant that I was damn near threatening the life of the president. I would definitely be comfortable tucking the bird shoot idea away on the small heap of "Couldn't Quite Pull It Offs."

But then Blake returned with his idea.

And I realized that it could actually work.

The question now was, how did we sell the rest of the graduating class on something so risky?

As it turned out, that part would not be as difficult as we'd anticipated.

———

THE COINCIDENCE that Willingham College had a falcon for a mascot was not lost on Blake. A bird from the birds, is how he billed it. That made it even more important that the idea go off without a hitch.

As he ran down everything to me, I was astonished at how much thought he had put into the idea's execution. I wondered briefly if he could have applied that same kind of focus to his schoolwork. He would have surely graduate summa cum laude then. He wasn't even graduating "Thank you, lawdy!" In fact, he was provisional, which meant he still had six credits to take after he marched across the stage in full academic regalia to accept an empty degree folder.

"It's like picking a pocket," he said, although we both knew he had never done that. "You have to distract a person by touching him in a place away from your primary target."

I listened, nodding my head, realizing he had a point. When I recounted the information to the other seniors, I knew we had struck pay dirt. The only thing we had to worry about was if any of the graduating seniors would snitch.

That was no small concern, either. Even Harriet Tubman had to carry a pistol and a pouch of opium when helping slaves sneak along the Underground Railroad. Interestingly, and much to everyone's surprise, not a soul leaked our plan.

That Sunday, donning our black robes, we sat patiently, our middle fingers itching.

————

WHEN BLAKE originally mentioned the idea to me, I had assumed he meant we would be shooting the bird to President Bush during his commencement speech. That would have been the most obvious choice—and the choice that would have surely gotten all of us expelled (if not more). That's not what we did, though.

Tickled with ourselves, we had all shot choreographed and enthusiastic birds, all at the same time, some people doing it with a left hand, other's with a right. We were so smooth with it that we went virtually unnoticed, as if nothing had even happened.

The only person from our graduating class who didn't shoot the bird that commencement morning was Blake. He alone took the photograph that verified what really happened. Using a high-speed film and a camera with a lightning quick shutter, he got off the single picture that would serve as proof of what we had done.

He would later show me the solitary 8x10" picture he had printed, commemorating the occasion.

I could still hear the college president's voice, as I studied the photograph: "Congratulations! You are now graduates of the class of 2005!"

In the distance, between our victoriously flying hats, lifting from our extended middle fingers, was a barely distinguishable George Walker Bush, a giant smile dancing upon his face.

AN OCCURRENCE AT OSCEOLA AVENUE

(A contemporary retelling of Ambrose Bierce's "An Occurrence at Owl Creek Bridge")

"I can't breathe," Jarius Jackson said, as he struggled to rotate his thick 6'3" body away from the bear-strength arms of the police officer behind him. "I need my inhaler!"

The officer jammed a knee into the back of Jarius's leg, causing Jarius to fall into a kneeling position. The sidewalk screamed at his kneecaps, which only intensified the burning in his lungs.

"Don't move!" the officer behind him shouted, and out the corners of his eyes, Jarius could see at least two other officers approaching him on either side, guns drawn. "I'm warning you, big guy. Stay down!"

Jarius wheezed hard, trying to take in as much air as he could. "Can't breathe!"

"He ain't even do nothin'!" a woman yelled from beyond the officers. "Y'all just want to mess with him 'cause he big and black. Shame on y'all!"

Jarius tried to lift his head to see the growing throng of people forming a semicircle around the police officers, but the burning in his chest was starting to draw his body into a ball.

"Everybody stand back!" one officer yelled.

"He already told y'all he can't breathe! Y'all gon' let that man die out here?" a guy in the crowd said.

Jarius felt the panic set in. He had only been without his inhaler once during an asthma attack, and he thought he was going to die. He survived that episode because his mother got him to breathe into a bag and calm himself until they could get to the local pharmacy and refill his prescription. Still it had been a close call. Not only were there not any paper bags around, he was acutely aware of the guns pointed in his direction.

The burning in his chest intensified with each breath he attempted. Maybe if he could just stand up and stretch, then he could get enough air to calm himself a bit. He just needed to summon the energy to get to his feet. His hands were outstretched and empty so there was no reason for the officers to think he was armed.

Jarius grunted hard, like the engine of an old car coming to life, and he began to rise, lifting the officer draped across his back with him. Just as he reached his full height he heard a loud, sharp popping sound. Startled, the excited crowd began to scatter. It was in this melee of animated bodies that Jarius took a deep breath and began to run.

He could barely feel his feet beneath him as he sprinted on the balls of his feet around the corner and down through an alley. He could hear the walkie-talkies and sounds of the police officers pursuing him, but he refused to look back. That's how you tripped and fell and let them catch you, he thought.

He reached the end of the alley and turned left, racing down the block. He could no longer feel the tightness in his chest as he ran. His adrenaline drowned out the pain. If he could just get home, he could get to his inhaler--but even more importantly, he could get to his wife. Osceola Avenue was roughly six blocks from his apartment. He was determined not to let anything stop him.

The crackle of the walkie-talkies persisted, so he cut right, racing through a courtyard between two large brownstones, and leaped a fence at the back of the enclosure. At this point, he could see his apartment building in the distance. In a flat-out sprint, Jarius propelled his body down the street, seeking to close the two-block distance with the strides of his long legs. He could no longer hear the police officers behind him. He patted his pockets, searching for his cell phone to call Yvette, but couldn't find it. It must have fallen out, he thought. But just ahead in the remaining block, Jarius could see her walking down the steps of the apartment building.

"Yvette!" he called out, running towards her.

She looked up and smiled.

With his arms outstretched, he closed the remaining distance and reached for the warmth of his wife's embrace.

Suddenly, the crack of a single gunshot pierced through the cacophony of police officers and onlookers on Osceola Avenue.

Jarius Jackson, who had just risen to his feet, fell forward, face-first, toward the concrete and into the waiting arms of his wife.

TO GET BREAD AND BUTTER

Bananas. Beef. Beer. Bread. Butter. I only shop for "B's" on the first Tuesday of the month.

Olson's Supermarket is located exactly 0.8 miles down Main Street from my two-bedroom townhouse, and it is nearly eleven o'clock at night on Tuesday, February 7th. I will make it to Olson's at eleven o'clock exactly, park on the side of the building in a space usually unoccupied and walk eight yards to the entrance of the store, where I will take the second shopping cart, gently sliding the first cart to the side. I will then proceed to the produce section located on the far right side of the store, working my way across each aisle to the next item on the list. It just so happens that each of my items is alphabetized and corresponds with the various aisles that progress toward the left side of the store. I buy bananas first and butter last, and it just so happens that butter and bread are on opposite sides of the same aisle. This system has worked for me for the last seven years, and I find it very comforting.

Rising from the sofa, I put on my lucky red Adidas warm-up jacket and lace up my matching red tennis shoes. I am now ready to go.

I step outside the back of my townhouse and begin walking towards my black Jeep Cherokee when I hear a voice call out in my direction.

"Raphael, hold on for a moment."

As I turn my head, I see my neighbor Gus walking slowly in my direction. I continue walking toward my Jeep, slowing just a little so that he might see that I have somewhere to be.

"Raphael," he says again, a bit winded from his attempt to move his slothful mass more quickly toward me.

As I open the door to my vehicle, I respond, "Yes, Gus. How are you doing?"

"Oh, I'm fine. Just wanted to let you know that I read your last book, the one about that treasure hunter."

"Thanks. I'm glad that you bought one of my books." I say, lifting my leg to enter the vehicle.

"Well, actually, I didn't buy it. I'm reading my girlfriend's copy." He reaches in his back pocket and pulls out a battered, dog-eared mass-market paperback book. It appears to be held together by a large bone colored rubber band, and I scarcely recognize it as a book at all.

I nod at Gus, attempting to excuse myself. I look down at my watch and see that it is 10:55

p.m. I have exactly five minutes to get to the grocery store. I take a seat in my Jeep, and as I reach
to close the door, Gus runs around to the side of
my vehicle and asks, "So maybe you could sign
this book for her—or me, since I'm your
neighbor."

I reach in my pocket to find one of the three
ballpoint black pens I keep there. He hands me
the mass of pages, and I remove the rubber band.
"What's your girlfriend's name, Gus?"

"Shelia. But make sure you put my name
down there too, and say something about us being
neighbors. That would be really cool."

I hurriedly scribble "to Shelia and Gus, the
best neighbors" and hand it back to him.

"Gee, thanks," Gus says. "So how's the new
book coming?"

I glance down at my watch again, and I have a
little over two minutes to make it to the store.

"Gus, you'll have to excuse me. I have to go
now."

"O.K. We'll talk later," he says, but I barely
hear him as I am already closing the door and
backing up the Jeep.

It's people like Gus who drive me completely
crazy! I was once married to a woman for all of
three months before we had to file for divorce.
Truthfully, I'm surprised we lasted that long. (I
guess that's what happens when you marry
someone you meet off of the Internet.) We cited
irreconcilable differences, but the truth was that

she couldn't deal with my need to maintain a certain type of order around me at all times, and I couldn't deal with her always threatening to mess up that order every time I looked up. She called me an obsessive-compulsive asshole. I called her a sloppy gold-digging bitch. To me, order promotes productivity, and with my occupation, I need a lot of order. Personally, I don't understand how anyone would want to go about his daily routine without some kind of structure.

Still bothered by Gus's slowing me down, I whip out of the parking lot with my foot pressed down on the gas, headed down Main Street. Up ahead of me, I can see the stoplight starting to change to yellow. I push down on the gas, and as the light turns red, I zoom through, nearly clipping a guy walking out into the middle of the street wearing dark colors. Can you believe that? Walking out in the street with dark colors on at night? What in the world was *he* thinking?

I arrive at my usual parking spot at exactly eleven, my heart still racing from the panic of nearly arriving late. I take a moment to catch my breath, but I can't wait too long because I have to be in the checkout line by 11:30, back home after that, and have everything completely put away by midnight. It has to be that way because I go to bed at midnight every night so that I can wake up at six o'clock in the morning to work do my ten pages for whatever book I'm working on.

I lock my door and walk briskly toward the

entrance of the store, and as I enter, I reach for the second shopping cart. I'm still thinking about the fact that I almost didn't make it on time because of Gus and that guy out in the middle of the road. Oh well, no harm, no foul.

I re-center myself.

Bananas. Beef. Beer. Bread. Butter.

I push my cart over to aisle one, Produce. Because I allow myself exactly thirty minutes to grocery shop for these items, I can take my time and find the absolute best products on the shelves. Tonight as I stand by the bananas, I move the ones on the top out of the way quickly. Too many hands have probably touched those. I find some greenish-yellow bananas that look to be very firm. They will ripen well over the next two or three days. Grabbing a plastic bag and tearing along the perforated edges, I slide the bundle of connected bananas into the bag, twisting the bag three complete revolutions to seal it. I place them in the cart and continue on toward the end of the aisle.

Beef is along the back wall, and while I could easily jump across the store to grab items, I tend to push my cart past each aisle, curious to see who else does their shopping this late at night. Often time it is college students or people getting off work from factory jobs. But as I pass aisle two, I notice that it is empty. No one getting pasta, rice, or spaghetti sauce tonight, I imagine.

I continue pushing my cart, and as I pass aisle three I notice a couple of teenagers making out by the canned soup. At the end of the aisle, near the front of the store, is a dark skinned, bearded old man facing in my general direction. I divert my attention back to the next item on my list, beef.

Reaching the refrigerated meat area, I sort through various packages of meat, looking for the leanest and finest cuts. Again, I find what I am looking for in a matter of minutes, and I am off in search of the next item.

Next is beer. Aisle seven.

As I pass aisle five, I glance down it. I see the old man again, this time standing next to the coffee section, eyes looking toward my end of the aisle. He looks at me and nods. I nod back. His frumpy blue Member's Only-style jacket is zipped tightly over his bulging stomach, and his large ears look as if they could have been slapped onto the side of his dark, hairy face. His beard is bushy and runs into the thickness of his nappy gray hair, leaving only his nose and eyes to be visible. I push on to the next aisle.

Standing closer up the aisle, I see the man again, this time standing next to the potato chips. I stop for a moment, shaking my head. Only then does it occur to me that this guy might be fol-lowing me. Is he a fan or a person with too much time on his hands? Maybe I'm still shaken up about nearly arriving late and I'm imagining this whole thing. The man, however, pulls down a bag of chips from the shelf and looks in my direction again, nodding. It is only at this point that I re-

alize that he doesn't have a shopping cart or bas-
ket. I nod uneasily in his direction and continue
pushing on.

I turn on to aisle seven for my Budweiser (if it
were my "M" day, it would be Miller). There
again, standing roughly ten feet down the aisle, is
the old man reaching for a case of sodas. I grab a
six-pack and pretend not to see him. To nod at
him a third time would be extremely awkward.
None of this makes sense to me. All I know is that
this man is making me deeply uncomfortable, but
I have to stick to my list though because time is of
the essence. Both the bread and butter are two
aisles over, so I push my cart back up the aisle to
the back of the store and make a left.

Passing aisle eight, I see the old man again.
This time he is much closer. I stop my cart dead in
its tracks, and before I realize it, my heart is now
racing in my chest. The man looks up from the
magazine he is holding and nods at me. This time
he smiles, peeling back his thick, cracked lips to
reveal dingy brown teeth.

I quickly back up my things to the previous
aisle, and glance down the aisle to find the same
man on that aisle but possibly farther away. I back
up another three aisles and the man is still there,
farther and farther toward the other end of the
aisle. By the time I make it back to the produce
section, the man is nowhere to be found.

I glance at my watch. It is 11:20 p.m. I have
exactly ten minutes to get my bread and butter

and make it to the checkout line. Although the grocery store is open twenty-four hours, I find it much easier to stay on my schedule. Already I am in danger of being thrown off, but I sense that once I make it to the last aisle, I can make up for lost time and still make it to the checkout before 11:30.

For a brief moment, I ponder taking the items that I have already picked up to the checkout, but I can't do that. I either get everything, or I get nothing. And getting nothing is not an option because I shop for my "C's" tomorrow at three o'clock p.m. That would destroy my entire schedule for the month if I left out of here tonight empty-handed.

I look across the store and realize that I am the only one on the rear aisle. I only have two items left to pick up, and as I look at my watch, I realize that I don't have the time to put off completing my task. If the man is going to be there, then, dammit, let him be, because I need to get in the checkout line by 11:30 p.m. It is already bad enough that I won't have the time to go through the bread like I want to, but getting to the checkout at the right time is really taking priority.

I gear back and start pushing my cart forward, slowly at first, and then faster, until I'm almost running with it across the store, straining to avoid glancing down the side aisles. I reach the end of the store and turn my cart left onto the last aisle.

It's empty!

I quickly grab the second loaf of whole wheat bread from the second shelf from the top, pushing the first one aside, before turning around to get the butter. When I turn around, I find myself staring face-to-face with the old man. His breath spills out from behind his wicked smile like garbage baked on a rock during the hottest day of summer. His skin is so dry that cracks run along his face into the depths of his matted beard. His eyes are a cloudy grey with a thick puss oozing out of the corners, and they are locked on me like some type of war missile.

I quickly jump back, straining to pull the cart between us to serve as a barrier, but the man blocks me and pushes me into the bread. I fall back, shocked. As I try to catch myself, my hand hits a soft loaf of bread and loses grip, causing me to fall onto the floor. The man quickly stands over me, and I find that I am too afraid to move. His bulk towers over me like a huge dark mountain, and before I realize it, he is reaching into my shopping cart, removing things. When he takes my choice steak and slings it down the aisle onto the floor so hard that it snaps loose of its plastic and lands facedown on the floor, my chest tightens.

Next, he hurls the bananas over the aisle onto the floor of the next aisle. I hear the thud of them hitting the ground. Now I can feel my breaths shortening.

All I can think is that I don't have enough time to replace the items before I run out of time.

The man takes my six-pack of beer out of the cart and tosses the cans on their sides, denting them. One can pops open and sprays the cookies next to the bread.

My cart is nearly empty, and as I try to stand up, I find that I can't catch my breath at all. I reach behind myself to find a shelf for support, but the old man takes my wheat bread and begins pelting me with it. The bag of bread slaps across my face like a backhand. Again I fall back. As I try to stand, the man slaps me back down with a gnarled, bony hand that feels like a brick wrapped in crusted flesh. The pain bolts across my cheek, burning into the side of my face.

"Help!" I yell, not wanting to surrender to the madness of what is going on around me but having little choice in the matter. I can barely hear my own voice, but I don't have the air to yell out again. The old man looks down at me, and fear races over me when I realize that for the first time in seven years I won't make my schedule. My head swimming, I fall back unconscious.

———

WHEN I COME TO, I find a pimply-faced red-headed boy, who could have been no more than twenty years old, kneeling down beside me. He's trying to assist me in sitting upright. The whole time I see his lips moving, but I can't make out what he's saying. The Olson's nametag on his shirt reads "Rusty." I look at him, straining my eyes against the fluorescent overhead lights of the aisle.

I watch his lips move, and I start to gradually make out what he is saying. "I'm sorry, mister," he repeats over and over.

My mind is muddled with thoughts of the old man and wondering what time it is. As I sit up, I frantically look around for the man. Rusty and I are the only ones on the aisle though. I look around for my bread and the dented cans of beer, but they are no longer there.

"I'm so sorry," Rusty says again.

"Rusty? Rusty, look, what's going on here? A man just assaulted me with food from my cart."

Rusty stops for a moment and looks at me, his eyebrows raised in an arch of curiosity. He doesn't seem to understand what I'm talking about, so I repeat it.

"Rusty, an old man just assaulted me in this store. I need for you to notify the authorities right now!"

"Sir," Rusty says. "I don't know what you're talking about."

"What do you mean?" I rise to my feet and look for my cart. It is resting off to the side of the aisle with a small bag of tied-up bananas, a package of choice steak, a loaf of bread, and a six-pack of Budweiser.

"There's no one else who's been over here. I

had just finished mopping the floor, and I forgot to put the sign down. I just started working here last week, and I can't take it if they fire me. I have a kid at home. Please, mister, if you're OK, let's just leave this between us."

I look at Rusty, and I can see in his eyes that he is genuinely scared. I touch my back and twist my waist to see if I'm all right. I don't feel any pain, but when I glance at my watch, I see that it's now 11:40 p.m.

My heart is aching now. I reach for my cart. "You know what, Rusty? I just want to get my stuff and get out of here. No harm, no foul, right?"

"Y-yes, sir," he responds and stands back from me.

I grab the first package of butter I come upon and push my cart toward the checkout. My stomach is all out of sorts, and my head is starting to hurt like hell. There is no line on the only open checkout lane, and when the cashier recognizes me, she tries to weigh my bananas and ring me up as quickly as possible. It's too little, too late though, and I'm already frustrated and upset, so I just reach in my pocket and pay her from the twenty I had folded three times and placed squarely across the bottom of my front right pocket.

My head feels like fireworks are going off inside my brain, and now I only want to go home and sleep off this night. I grab the paper bag, tucking it in my arms like a toddler, and I walk out the store into the cool night. Each step I take is heavy and my vehicle seems so far away. The cars drifting randomly through the night don't even register to me.

I place the bag on the backseat of my Jeep, plopping myself down in the driver seat. I feel as if all of the wind has been snuffed out of my sails. I can't explain why I feel so dejected. I just do. I feel dirty and worthless. I only want to get home now and be inside the safe confines of my own home. Everything just feels totally out of sync.

I crank up the vehicle and pull out of the parking lot. My eyes are heavy, and I find myself almost completely consumed in disappointment, so much so that it takes me a moment to recognize the heat and stench rising from my backseat, signaling that I am not alone. I look in the rearview mirror and am horrified to see the old man, sitting hunched over, quietly tossing my groceries out of the window into the dark street.

THE VOYEUR

The old man eased from the shadows, his motions both fluid and easy, as he lifted the camcorder into the sunlight. He adjusted the optical zoom, and just as he aimed it at the top of the building, the child stepped into view. The flowing satin fabric caught on the slight breeze, and damned if the kid didn't really look like a superhero. The child placed his fists on either side of his waist and poked out his chest, taking in the moment. It was a thing of beauty, the old man thought while recording.

The boy stepped to the edge of the building, his golden locks shifting with the wind.

"You have to believe," the old man whispered under his breath, adjusting his camcorder. He looked away for a moment to the group of children gathering below. They were doing just as he had instructed them. Now the *real* crowd would come.

A woman looked upward and screamed, triggering a chain reaction among the swelling crowd.

"Someone call 9-1-1!" a man yelled.

The old man quickly lowered his camcorder to get a shot of the growing crowd, before returning his gaze to the boy who stood frozen like a statue atop the building. He could scarcely make out the boy's face, but it was clear the boy's posture and stance betrayed his ten-year-old body.

Then the boy moved. It was a slight half-step, but everyone, including the old man, gasped collectively. It was a delicious moment, this child weighing his power over this world, his ability to transcend gravity and give himself over to his dreams. The old man smiled, his hand perspiring behind the camcorder.

And without warning, the boy leapt off the building, his cape catching in the wind and trailing boldly behind him as he outstretched his arms so that his body became parallel with the earth. It was a beautiful sight, thought the old man, as he moved his camera with the child. The boy *could* really fly!

But in the brief seconds of the boy's commitment to flight, gravity wrapped its heavy hands around him, yanking him to the earth with such violent force that the boy seemed to disintegrate into a bloody dust as his body slammed against the concrete.

When the old man later replayed the video, he admired that fleeting moment of the boy, prostrate against the wind, oblivious to the screams below, floating just off the roof of the building, his cape rippling perfectly behind him. He only hoped that the other children would be equally inspired. Surely there was one among them who viewed himself as bulletproof or capable of breathing under water.

Pausing the video just before the child hit the sidewalk below, the old man smiled at the intensity of the child's face.

That boy was determined to fly—even until the very end.

THE BOX

G rowing up, I would hear stories of the old woman who lived at the end of the street and how she kept a man's soul in a box. It wasn't until years later that I realized I had never laid eyes on the woman and that the entire thing was probably some urban legend that had about as much gravity as an episode of *Tales From The Crypt*. And I was prepared to leave well enough alone, that is until I happened to catch her leaving her house one day.

I couldn't believe my eyes. For seventeen years, before I went to college, I had never seen her, but now that I was home for the Christmas break during my senior year of college, I had somehow happened to chance upon her. Returning from my mailbox, I saw a small, withered shape moving roughly thirty yards away from me. I turned and stared, like people do when they find themselves passing a car accident. The little old woman was pale, her hair a chalky white. She moved about slowly towards a large black car parked in her yard. I watched in amazement, thinking to myself that there was no way such a small elderly woman could maneuver such a large machine.

Once she started up her car, I hopped into my own and decided to follow her. Struggling to keep a safe distance, so as to not alert her, I hung back more than half a block, just enough to keep her in sight. While tailing her, it occurred to me that what I was doing bordered on stupid, but in a small town like Daily, where there wasn't much to do on Saturdays, no one could really blame me.

She parked at the Kroger grocery store, and as she exited her car, I cruised by her very slowly. In my rear view mirror, I could see the deeply drawn lines of age peeling back from her beady eyes. Her hair, tucked beneath a red knitted toboggan, was nearly the same color as her powdery face. But it was her eyes—*those eyes*—that reflected what I perceived as evil. Not like the evil of a master villain though. More like the glint of evil in a kid's eye before he proceeds to pull the legs off of a small insect. And that image of the old woman stayed with me, long after she had gone into the grocery store.

———

GROWING up I had often confused the word "coincidence" with the word "irony." I think I preferred the latter because it sounded better, but it took me getting back a paper during my freshman year of college to realize that the two were, in fact, not synonymous. My composition professor wrote a nice little note in the margin of one of my papers stating something to the effect that a coincidence was a concurrent thing with no seeming connection, while an irony was something happening that was the opposite of what might have been expected. Only through repeated error did I eventually latch on to this concept. However, while surfing the website several days after the Kroger episode, I stumbled across something that I had trouble categorizing as either a coincidence or an irony.

I had been looking at a photo gallery on a website dealing with the Jim Crow era. Being that a number of the pictures in the online gallery were pictures of lynchings, I had painfully explored them, absorbing all of the details that surrounded each of the victims as they met their demises. Often I was so saddened that I could scarcely move to the next photograph. As I neared the end of that section of the exhibition, I stumbled upon yet another public lynching. This one, however, seemed a bit odd. I stared at the picture for several minutes before I began to recognize the buildings in the background. It was the Humma County Courthouse, and surrounding the hanged victim, who I could not even identify (either due to the quality of the black and white photograph or the fact that he had been beaten so badly—probably both), I noticed the large assembly of white people, many of whom I figured were either now living their last days in nursing homes or had managed to pass along their racists beliefs to their children and grandchildren. A chill went over me as I allowed this notion to sink in.

Ironically, or *coincidentally*, one of the women featured in the picture had the same beady eyes that I had seen on the old woman in the grocery store parking lot. I stared at the face, retracing in my mind the old woman's appearance in my rearview window. There were not many things in this life that I was certain of, but I was convinced that the two women (the old woman and the woman in this picture) were one in the same.

Only then did I begin to take the stories about the box more seriously. I found myself obsessing over it during the day and dreaming about it at night. Was there really a man's soul in the box, and if so, was it the black man in the photograph I had seen? The eeriness of what I had discovered haunted me, and I felt like a man trying to outrun his own shadow against the blaze of the sun. I was restless and confused and, at times, tormented by my own curiosity. It was only then that I knew what I had to do.

———

THE DECISION TO break into the old woman's house was not a decision I toiled over for very long. It seemed like the only natural option for resolving this issue and bringing myself some kind of peace.

For roughly two weeks I watched her house, looking for patterns, any movements that would help me to understand her daily habits. It didn't take me long to realize that she lived alone. Another thing that I noticed was that she would often leave her house at ten o'clock every morning and drive the mile and half to the post office. Unlike my family, she did not receive her mail at her actual house. It normally took her ten minutes to do this routine; however, I noticed on Thursdays that she would stop by Kroger to pick up groceries, always leaving with two plastic bags. On those days she would take close to forty minutes to run her errands. Once I had gotten her schedule committed to memory, I took some time to refresh myself on how to jimmy open door locks, a skill I had picked up after locking my keys in my dorm room one too many times. If the old woman had an alarm on her house, I would just resort to my tried and true method for handling major crises: run like hell.

At times I contemplated whether I should just leave well enough alone, but then the image of the lynching would come to mind, and I would remind myself that my purpose was far too noble to abandon. I was going to get to the bottom of all of this, and if there was in fact a box in the house, I was going to open it and release its contents to the world.

On the Thursday morning that I had picked to break into the old woman's house, I woke up early and exercised in my bedroom. After getting myself warmed up, I messed with the morning crossword puzzle in the daily newspaper for a while. I wanted to make sure that I was operating on all cylinders when I went to the old woman's house.

At around 9:55 a.m., I walked outside and pretended to go check the mailbox. As I walked slowly, watching for the old woman, she came out like clockwork. I stood at the mailbox, pretending to peer inside while using my peripheral vision to see the old woman start up the old black car and pull out onto the road. My back was to her as she passed by, headed to the corner stop sign. When she turned onto Main Street, I walked briskly to the end of the street and cut back along the back of the house in such a sly motion that I was impressed with myself. Before I knew it, I was standing at the backdoor of the woman's house already jimmying the lock loose. When I twisted open the door, I could hear nothing more than the central air unit buzzing quietly. The dimness of the room, coupled with the thick, choking smell of mothballs reminded me that I was on foreign soil and had to move quickly.

The backdoor was by the kitchen, so I tiptoed through the kitchen, through the dining area, into the main room. As I turned, I saw a small hallway with several doors along each side. I worked myself quickly down the hall to an open door on the right. The thick quilt lying at the foot of the bed made me question whether or not I had found the right room. I went in anyway.

With my heart beating in my stomach (a feeling far worse than butterflies), I combed the dresser. Next to the vanity mirror was a jewelry box opened up to reveal small gold and pearl accessories. If I wanted to rob this woman, I would have made out like a bandit. Instead, I looked for *the* box, suddenly realizing I had no idea of what it looked like. I guess I had just assumed I would find it and automatically recognize it. A matter of fate and faith, if you will.

As furiously as I searched the room, I quickly realized that I might have been totally mistaken in breaking into this woman's house. I looked at my watch and then walked over by the window in the room, unlocking it. If something happened and I needed to make a dash, I would have the window as a way out. Again, I stared around the room, looking aimlessly for anything that seemed odd, which, depending on the circumstances, would have included nearly everything in the house. It must be in the other room, I thought. Just as I started to dash across the hallway, I heard the old car pulling back into the driveway.

A sudden heat flushed around my face as the thought of being caught became a stark reality. If I didn't find what I was looking for, I would have to come back again, and I didn't know if I had the courage to repeat this adventure. Hearing her closing the door, I looked around the room again, quickly taking in one last glance at my surroundings. On the top shelf of the open closet, I saw an odd looking box, faded red velvet peeling away. The box was larger than a ring box, but smaller than one that might contain a bracelet. I quickly grabbed it, lifted the window and crawled halfway through before I felt something brush my leg.

I looked down to see a cat meandering around my leg. Hearing the door open, I slid through the window, landing on the ground. Quickly I pulled the window down and eased my way along the side of the house back to the street.

Had anyone seen me? I didn't think so. I prayed they didn't.

All I wanted to do was get back to my bedroom and open the box.

———

SITTING BACK on my bed with the box resting in my hands, I rattled it slightly. I could hear something inside, but whatever it was, it was not very heavy. Maybe I had picked the right box. Maybe this was the man's soul. But did a soul rattle around in box when you shook it?

I lifted the lid carefully and placed it on the bed next to me. As I stared at the object, I was confused. What the hell was I looking at? It looked like a dark piece of leather, not different than what one might affix to a keychain. I picked it up, noticing how delicate it felt in my fingers. It was smooth and dark, and I rolled it around between my fingers until I began to notice some markings on the object. One end looked uneven, while the other looked as if it had a small thin plastic tip, a handle or something. And for a moment, I resigned to myself that I was even more confused by this object than I might have been by anything else I had seen in the old woman's house.

Only when I continued playing with this object did my eyes peel back and reveal to me the actual visual of my own hands wrapped around it. At that point, I wondered why I had not noticed it before. I quickly dropped the object back into the box, my hands shaking, as I realized that I had just been holding a man's horribly mutilated finger.

———

I BURIED the finger in my backyard. It seemed like the right thing to do. But what had the old woman been doing with it in her closet? Was it a souvenir from a lynching? I had no clue, and I realized that I had only opened the door for even more questions.

I would like to believe that I liberated what was left of one man's remains and, by doing so, put his soul at rest. That's what I want to believe, but I'm not very sure about anything anymore. The old white man at the hardware store. Was he in the picture too? Or the white woman who refused to touch my hand while giving me back change at the grocery store. Was she a child of one of the people in the picture?

When I returned to school for the spring semester of my senior year, I had trouble forgetting my town and what I had experienced that winter. I guess it is no wonder that I accepted an internship in New York for the summer and ended up relocating to Brooklyn that fall.

When I hear people talk about the South, I think about that red box, and realize that I will always have a love/hate relationship with my home.

HEAVY

The box was much smaller than Sean had expected. It could have easily contained a small watch, not the ashes of a human being. Well, not the entire human being. His father had requested his remains be cremated and sent to everyone in the family, all ten of them, including Sean's mother.

Once he opened it, he realized the box was generously larger than the actual remains. His mother had sent them using regular postage, nothing special. She had no fond affections for her late husband, which everyone knew. Still, Sean thought she might have spent a little more money on honoring his father's last wishes, especially with the insurance money she had received. If his father had not died from lung cancer as a result of working twenty-five years in the shipyard, Sean would not have put it past his mother to lace his father's coffee with cyanide.

The remains rested inches in front of him, on

the counter, in a small plastic bag sealed with a rubber band. It was less than a handful of grayish sand that could have once been an arthritic elbow or a bum knee or a calloused foot.

In that moment Sean wanted to do something respectful to honor his father's remains, but his mind was blank. His father had never supported his life choices and had made little effort to get to know Sean's wife, Liza, during the four years they had been married. When they found out they were expecting, they decided not to tell his father, who by then had been moved to a hospice to live out his final days on morphine. Sean was thankful Liza was away visiting her sister because he didn't want to have to deal with his father's remains in front of her.

He closed his eyes as he held the small bag in his hands. It could have been a few spoonfuls of sugar, the lightness of it. His father, the hard man, heavy in every sense of the word, now reduced to grains that could easily blow away into nothingness.

Sean wondered what his siblings were going to do with their ashes, what his mother would do with hers. It was then that he noticed a slip of paper inside the box, a note from his mother: "Do with these as you please. I have already flushed mine. Love, Mom."

He stared numbly at his father's ashes, fully grasping the hate the man had inspired in others. Sean didn't think he would flush the remains—no one deserved that level of disrespect, he figured—but he might find a beautiful spot, somewhere off the bay, where he could release them into the wind, a place beautiful enough to hopefully heal the darkness of an atrophied soul.

TOWERS

I haven't been to the promenade in Brooklyn Heights in nearly twenty years, and much has happened since then. Sometimes I still feel like the same guy I was then—or maybe I'm just tempted to act that way when I start romanticizing my past. Even as I step off the subway at Clark Street, iPhone earbuds nestled in my ears with the sounds of Roy Ayers, I am reliving the first time Eva and I made love.

Our first date was on this promenade, just four short blocks from the apartment I was living in at the time. She was working as a singer at a theme restaurant in Midtown Manhattan, and while she was on one of her fifteen minute breaks, we somehow or another found ourselves conversing about our common Southern heritage. I asked for her number (so that we could keep in touch), but I knew the moment she lifted her pen from the back of that receipt I was going to ask her out.

She accepted, and that Saturday she arrived to me via the 2-Train. The promenade was the first place we headed.

The cool October air caused us to huddle together, her body eventually falling into my embrace, as we cast our gazes along the East River, admiring the Twin Towers that punctuated the transitioning sky of blues, violets, and purples. The Brooklyn Bridge stood off to our right, the Statue of Liberty to our left. In that moment, I could feel my heart wanting to love her, needing only the slightest of reasons to break free and declare itself. But I was cool, figuratively and literally, and I held her so close to me that our cheeks touched.

"Will you sing for me?" I asked, remembering how her voice had captivated me at the restaurant.

She smiled, and even in the brilliant bronze hue of her skin, I could see her blush. I smiled in turn, figuring that her being a professional singer would not have made her blush, but my presence might have. I hoped so anyway.

"What do you want me to sing?" she asked.

"I don't know. Anything, I guess."

"Well, what's your favorite song?"

I could have easily told her anything, because all I wanted to do was hear her sing, but for some reason, my mind started to fan through my entire music catalog. Favorite song? I had never considered such a thing, not with all of the CDs that I had amassed.

She turned to face me, and from out of nowhere I blurted, "My Funny Valentine." I don't know if it was because I owned at least ten different versions of the song or if it was because I thought it was standard enough for her to know. Maybe it was because I loved the quirky lyrics and enjoyed the idea of her singing those lyrics to me. I sat back, awaiting her response.

As her lips parted and her rich alto voice entered the space between us, I knew I wanted her more than any woman I had ever known.

"Your looks are laughable, unphotographable," she sang. "Yet you're my favorite work of art."

In that interminable moment that she sang to me, I felt as if my body had become an instrument and she was the virtuoso whose voice pushed every cell of my body into chords that rhythmically and melodically made me a part of her art.

By the time she finished, the butterflies in my stomach were flapping their wings wildly. A "that was good" just didn't seem to be adequate—not when all I wanted to do was kiss her. As soon as she closed her mouth, I made my move. My eyes were already sealed and the gentle scent of her perfume seemed to beckon me forward. I was so committed to the kiss that it took me a moment to register that both of her hands were planted firmly against my chest, freezing me in my tracks.

I opened my eyes, unable to hide my stinging pride.

"What are you looking for?" she asked.

"What do you mean? I was looking for a kiss. I see you standing here, beautiful in this sunset, and I want to be closer to you."

"Closer to me how?"

The butterflies stopped flapping, formed into a ball and dropped down into my stomach. The realization that I would have to probably explain what I was feeling, before I even understood it myself, made me wish I could disappear into the cool breeze tickling my nose, making me feel for a second that I might actually sneeze my affections into Eva's face.

"I'm just really feeling you."

She nodded, considering my words.

"Well, let me ask you a question," I added. "Are you in a position to entertain my feelings?"

"Is that your way of asking if I have a boyfriend?"

"I guess so."

"I'm single, but I have to be selective."

"Being selective's a good thing."

"It's just that I have gone out with more knuckleheads than I care to mention, and they all start out real cool, saying the right things, doing the right things. Then somewhere along the way, they flip the script on me. I just can't handle any more of that stuff. Not right now."

"I'm not trying to game you or anything," I said. "In fact, if you're really interested in getting to know me, we can take to it as slow as you'd like."

And we eventually did.

Our relationship moved so slowly that I feared I wouldn't be able to stay the course. Dating Eva required a Zen-like focus, and I was still young and restless, but she was perfect, if ever there were such a thing. Now as I turn my eyes toward the bridge on my right, I realize now more than ever that Eva was my *one*. I squandered two years of our relationship, simply because I wasn't ready to be in a relationship that consumed so much of my attention. Ironically, though, I feel I could be more than committed to her at this point in my life.

Or maybe I'm feeling that way because I'm standing here remembering that first date, the one that ended pleasantly with that soft, short kiss she planted upon my lips, just as we were turning to leave. Maybe when I turn to leave today I will no longer feel the sting of it all, wondering how her marriage is going (it's been nearly seven years), whether or not she has any children, or why she refuses to add me as a friend on Facebook, even after all of this time.

I have been chasing the idea of her for so long, wanting to find a woman with only a portion of what it is that Eva had to offer. I miss her in the stillest of moments, when my heart whispers through its loneliness its vow to never take a love like hers for granted again.

Even though she's moved on, I find myself unable to move beyond all of the memories. I am stuck in this emotional purgatory. Standing on this sacred ground, I hold fast to a moment that happened too many days ago to count.

I reach out, grasping the iron fence in front of me, watching the sun cling to the last moments of dusk. The skyline here is now altered, the Twin Towers having come down more than ten years ago. There is no longer any punctuation along the landscape, only an emptiness that might go unnoticed by anyone who has never stood in this spot before.

I can't take my eyes away from it.

"Crazy, isn't it," an older man says, sidling up next to me.

He runs a frail hand through what's left of his hair, his gaze also cast longingly across the East River.

"But you know what?" He places a finger to his chest, near his heart. "We're still here. Don't you get it? We're still standing."

THE WILL

I had never heard of Everett Carter before. My wife and I had just moved back to Mississippi to be closer to her folks, and I hadn't been an attorney at Sails & Associates all that long. But if I had known that my world would unravel overnight because of this man, I would have thought twice about representing him.

That Thursday wasn't that different from any other day. I had settled two of my personal injury cases, so I was in pretty good spirits. Sipping on my afternoon Sprite, I perused a file that Grady Sails, the senior partner, had placed on my desk during lunch. With it already being 3:30 in the afternoon, I knew I would probably be better off getting started on it the next day.

"Mr. Rush," my receptionist's voice rang out over my phone intercom.

I picked up the phone resting beside my computer. "Yes, Brandi?"

"We have a walk-in. Do you have anyone with you right now?"

"No."

"Well, you're the only attorney available. Would you like to meet with him?"

"Do you know what it's about?" I asked.

"He said that he just needed to get a will done."

I paused, looking at the file on my desk. I considered the fact that I had to prepare a report for Grady the next day listing the cases I had settled this month, including chancery matters like wills and deeds, that I had handled. This walk-in was a will, and depending on its complexity, it was possibly something that I could add to my weekly report. "Okay," I said. "Take him to the conference room."

The first thing I noticed about Everett Carter, once he had introduced himself, was his appearance. He was a heavyset elderly white man, clean-shaven, wearing a flannel shirt and a pair of faded denim overalls. His eyes were sharp beneath his bushy eyebrows. While Sails & Associates was a firm of black lawyers, at least sixty percent of our clients were rural white people, so Mr. Carter's presence in our office was hardly unique.

As he took a seat across the table from me, I inquired about what assets he wanted to dispose of in his will.

"I've figured that all out," he said, his raspy

voice tinged in a Southern drawl. "I want to leave everything to my son Tyrell Stewart."

I picked up the legal pad situated in the center of the table and began making notes. "Do you have property? Personal effects that you'd like to list?"

"Nope. Everything I own in this world, land and personal effects included, I want to go to my son Tyrell."

"Do you have any other family members?"

"Why do you ask?"

"Well, if Tyrell was your only surviving family member, you could easily deed the real property over to him now and maintain a life estate for yourself to avoid having it probated when you pass on."

"A life estate?"

"Yes. That means you will continue to live there while he technically owns it. That way you can give it away and continue living there for the rest of your life, all in one document," I responded.

"Oh," he said, reflecting over my remark. "I still want to do a will."

I nodded.

"Can you finish it today before the close of work?" Mr. Carter asked.

I looked up from my notepad. "Well, that's not usually our policy, but because your will is very simple, I could try to get right to it. I just need to get a little more information from you and find another person to serve as a witness."

"I'd really appreciate it," he said.

I could see in his eyes that he really wanted to make sure that the will got done that day. I wanted to ask him if he was expecting to die, but I thought such a question would be in poor taste. Instead, I excused myself and took the notepad back to my office to pull up a template for a will on my computer. I typed in the information I had taken down from Mr. Carter and printed out a copy of the document to review. Everything looked good, so I walked back to the reception area. I asked Brandi if she would come in and serve as a witness. I figured since she was from the next town over, she would have no connection to the client, which it turned out she didn't. She knew as much about Mr. Carter as I did, which was to say absolutely nothing.

As we entered the conference room, Mr. Carter was seated quietly in his chair, observing the generic artwork that adorned the cream col-ored walls.

"I need for you to read this and see if we need to make any changes before you sign it," I said, pushing the document in front of him.

He eyed it carefully, nodding as he read each line. Once he finished, he smiled at me and said, "Very good! So I just sign right here?"

"Yes. And Brandi and I will sign where it says 'Witnesses.'"

Mr. Carter made out a check for the amount I quoted him and asked me if I could take his copy of the will and have it placed in the vault at the chancery clerk's office in the Humma County Courthouse. Although it was not uncommon for my clients to request that copies of their wills be placed in the chancery clerk's vault for safekeeping, I had never experienced the request to take *the original* and have it locked away. I agreed though and gave him a receipt for his check. With only fifteen minutes left until five o'clock, I briskly walked the one and half block distance to the courthouse, arriving just as the deputy clerks were shutting down their computers.

As I approached the desk, Lance Tucker, the chancery clerk, approached me. "What can I do for you today, Attorney Rush?"

I handed him Mr. Carter's will, and he took it in his hands, examining it. "I need for you to place this in your vault, if that's not a problem."

He continued examining the document, and I wondered if he had even heard me, so I repeated myself.

"Oh. Of course," he responded, lifting the document in the air as if to signal that it would be in safe hands.

"Thanks," I said, walking out of the office and back to my own.

I had no idea that my world would come unglued the next day.

———

I NORMALLY ARRIVED at my office in the morning around eight, but that Friday morning, I arrived roughly fifteen minutes later. When I reached my desk, I noticed a message written in Brandi's bubbly handwriting for me to call an attorney by the name of Gerald Gibbons. The note said that whatever the matter was about, it was "VERY IMPORTANT!!!" The problem with Brandi was that every call that came from an attorney was considered "very important," and she had overused the exclamation marks to the point that they had little, if any, effect on how I read her messages. I left my office and fixed a cup of coffee before returning to my desk. Just as I sat down and eased my back into the softness of my chair, the phone rang.

"Yes?" I said, picking up the phone.

"Attorney Gibbons is on Line One for you, Mr. Rush."

"Okay," I responded, placing the phone down.

Quickly, I fanned through my mental Rolodex to try to figure out who this guy was. I didn't recall sending any letters to a "Gibbons." Maybe he was an associate working with one of the lawyers I had an ongoing case with. I hated when lawyers did this: trying to catch you off guard with phone calls from people you'd never spoken with. I had already decided to make the phone call brief due to a deposition or something. I'd figure out the exact nature of the lie once I got on the phone.

"Hello? Rush speaking."

"Mr. Rush? This is Gerald Gibbons, attorney for the Carter family, and I just wanted to ask if you had a burning desire to get disbarred, because what you're trying to pull off will not only get your license stripped, but you could see some serious jail time."

"Whoa! Slow down," I said, flustered. "Come again?"

"I've been asked by the family to look into the little stunt you pulled yesterday."

I paused, still trying to figure everything out. "Carter? As in Everett Carter?"

"Don't play games, Mr. Rush. The family is in bereavement, and your callous actions are only making them more and more upset."

"Okay, Mr. Gibbons, you obviously know something that I don't, so you'll need to fill me in on what you're talking about."

"I take it that you haven't watched the news this morning."

"No. Can't say that I have. This is normally the time when I read the paper."

"Well, Mr. Carter passed away last night."

I stared blankly at my computer screen. "Did he commit suicide?"

"Are you kidding me? He's been in a coma for the last three months since his stroke!"

I stood up slowly, leaning over my desk with the phone pinned between my ear and shoulder.

"I just saw Mr. Carter yesterday."

"No, you didn't. Mr. Carter hasn't been conscious in months. Needless to say, the family is very upset about you preparing that will, and they're contemplating suing you, especially since you have it in there that he's giving all of his property to some little black fella."

I puzzled over everything Gibbons was telling me, and none of it made sense. Then I wondered how he had found out about the will in the first place. Clearly the chancery clerk had called him shortly after I had dropped off the will. Something seemed very strange, and I was eager to get to the bottom of it.

In the Sunday paper, there was a huge spread about Everett Carter, and for the first time it hit me just what a big deal this all was. The words literally leapt off the page: "Local Millionaire Succumbs." There was a large picture of Mr. Carter, clad in a tuxedo, accepting some award from the local Chamber of Commerce. It was definitely the same man who had come into my office. The same bushy eyebrows and clean-shaven face. As far as I was concerned, Mr. Carter must have woken up from his coma, gotten dressed, and come down to my office to get the will done without anyone knowing. Maybe that's why he was wearing overalls and flannel. And maybe that's why he selected me, since I was not a native of Humma County and wouldn't have known him from a hole in the wall.

———

THE FOLLOWING DAY, I was subpoenaed for a hearing concerning issues with Mr. Carter's will. On the day of the hearing, I took one of the office copies of Mr. Carter's will, as well as a copy of the check that we kept on file. I even asked Brandi, who was equally clueless, to come with me, in the event that I needed to have her there.

After being sworn in, Gibbons lit into me as if I had stolen his child's trust fund. He asked me if I was aware of Mr. Carter's standing in the community. My ignorance of such a thing seemed tragically amplified in such a setting. He then inquired if I was aware that Mr. Carter had been comatose for nearly three months. After attempting to thoroughly embarrass me, I offered a copy of the will and the canceled check. I could have been handing him toilet paper for how little attention he paid these records. Looking at the faces of the four preppy white young adults identified as Mr. Carter's children, I knew that all they wanted was blood.

After being publicly roasted, the judge, a thin redheaded man who appeared to be in his forties, called both Gibbons and me into his chamber.

"Mr. Rush, if I didn't know better, I would think that you consciously created those documents to slander the good name of Everett Carter. Do you have any proof that Mr. Everett actually got up from his sick bed to come to your office?"

"Your honor, I have his check to my office, the signed will, and even the other witness whose signature is on the document. I'm pretty sure a handwriting analyst could verify the signature and settle this matter with ease. In all honesty, your Honor, that's more than enough to prove my case."

"I'll be the judge of that," he responded sternly.

"Your Honor," Gibbons said. "I am the family attorney for the Carters. I prepared Everett's will five years ago, and if he had wanted to make any changes, he would have surely called me. Also, lest I remind you, your Honor, I have sworn affidavits from the nurses and doctors at Humma County Hospital stating that Everett could not have gotten out of his bed. In fact, the medical records reflect that he never regained consciousness after his stroke and died peacefully. If we are to believe what Mr. Rush says, then Everett got out of his bed and went down to the office of some attorney he'd never dealt with to get a will done in which he left everything to some kid, whom I believe is African-American. It makes absolutely no sense at all, your Honor."

"I'm inclined to agree," the judge said. "Mr. Rush, I believe that this is a deliberate attempt to smear the name of an upstanding citizen of this great community. I am going to formally recommend charges be brought against you by the state bar and that you are prosecuted to the highest extent of the law."

I stared at the both the judge and Gibbons, my jaw agape. At that moment, it dawned on me that I was the only face of color in the judge's chamber. It all started to make sense to me, and I wanted to protest out of anger, but the thought of being held in contempt was not what I wanted. I figured I would just have to take my fight to the appellate level.

———

APPARENTLY GIBBONS or the judge had some pull with the ethics committee, and I was publicly reprimanded, where I had to go before the same judge in Humma County to have charges of my "dishonest behavior" read allowed and recorded for posterity. My disbarment followed closely on the heels of the reprimand. They never attempted to prosecute me though, maybe because they knew that my evidence would have held up if the thin light of justice had ever entered the courtroom.

———

A YEAR LATER, while I was teaching a few courses at the Humma County Community College, I was combing through my roll on the first day of class. Right there, near the top of the roll, was the name "Tyrell Carter." When I called his name, he said quietly, "Present." His light complexion, sandy hair, and bushy eyebrows left me little reason to suspect he was anyone other than who I thought he was. He was dressed simply, a large white t-shirt and a pair of natty, worn jeans, his canvas Converse sneakers tearing around the soles.

I wanted to tell him what had happened with Everett and the Carter family battles in court, but it all seemed like a sour footnote for a history both of us had been written out of. Plus, I was pretty sure that he knew well the details that had scandalized the town only a year earlier.

Once the class ended, I approached him. "If you have any problems with this class, don't hesitate to let me know. We are going to get through this together. Okay?"

"Okay," he responded, nodding his head and disappearing into the thick throng of students roaming the halls.

ACKNOWLEDGMENTS

First, I would like to thank my wife, Lauren, and my daughter, Zoë, for supporting my writing. It's not an easy thing to be the family of a writer, but they carry the burden well.

Next, I would like to thank my colleagues and students at Hampton University. I continue to grow as both a writer and a professor because I am blessed to be a part of such a supportive community.

I'd like to thank my extended family and my friends who continue to push me to tell more stories and preserve storytelling as an art form for the next generation.

Special thanks to Tayari Jones for being a good friend and mentor, Sabin Prentis for always having my back, Shonda Buchanan for encouraging me to continue the path I have charted, Elizabeth "Meatmumma" Stokes for her friendship and love, Richard Wall for just being an all around great friend and fellow writer, and Joi & Dawayne

Whittington for all of their support throughout the years.

Thank you to my parents. They put books into my hands at an early age and continue to be my biggest fans.

Thank you to my brother, Torrey. You continue to amaze and inspire me. Keep blazing new trails. And to my new sister-in-law, Sarah: you are a wonderful addition to our family, and we love you.

Because I write stories set in both large cities and small towns, I would like to thank my friends ranging from New York City down to West Point, Mississippi, for teaching me different ways of viewing the world.

Finally, I would like to thank those of you who have supported my writing throughout the years. Your continued support of my writing is what helps me to create new stories.

Peace.

Ran

Ran Walker is the author of six novels, two novellas, two short story collections, and a collaborative book with Sabin Prentis. His short stories and poetry have appeared in a variety of anthologies.

Ran is a graduate of Morehouse College (BA in English), Pace University (MS in Publishing), and George Washington University Law School (JD) and is the recipient of both a 2005 Mississippi Arts Commission/NEA artist grant and a 2006 artist mini-grant. He has also served as an Artist-in-Residence with the Commission. In addition, he is a past participant in the Hurston-Wright Writers Week Workshop and is the recipient of a fellowship from the Callaloo Writers Workshop.

His novel *Mojo's Guitar* was translated by renowned French translator Philippe Loubat-Delranc and was published in April 2015 by Éditions Autrement as *Il était une fois Morris Jones*.

Ran is an Assistant Professor of English and Creative Writing at Hampton University and lives in Virginia with his wife and much better half, Lauren, and his amazing little rockstar daughter, Zoë.

For More Information
www.ranwalker.com
ranwalker@icloud.com

www.ingramcontent.com/pod-product-compliance
Lightning Source LLC
Chambersburg PA
CBHW070312120726
47910CB00007B/2454